Praise for *Cross My Heart,*
THE HIDDEN DIARY, book 1

Cross My Heart was *very* descriptive (but not, like, overloaded!) and fun. It's a touching story that a lot of girls can relate to because of their own busy parents. I liked the mystery, too!

> Lilly, eleven years old, daughter of Liz Curtis Higgs,
> author of *Bad Girls of the Bible*

Mama mia! *Cross My Heart* was a great book! I liked the way the author left you hanging at the end of each chapter. It made you want to keep reading. I could really relate to some of the characters, and Claudette made me laugh. You'll love this book! Cross my heart!

> Tavia, ten years old, daughter of Deborah Raney,
> author of *A Vow to Cherish* and *Beneath a Southern Sky*

This book was really good, interesting, and fun. I couldn't say I had one favorite part because I loved the whole book! I couldn't put it down.

> Tyler, eleven years old, daughter of Lisa E. Samson,
> author of *The Church Ladies*

I couldn't put this book down! I guarantee you'll love *Cross My Heart,* and it will keep you on the edge of your seat.

> Marie, thirteen years old, daughter of Terri Blackstock, author
> of the NEWPOINTE 911 series

Cross My Heart is a very exciting book. Lucy . . . meets new friends and learns about God. I know my friends will love this book like I did. Maybe we'll find a hidden diary somewhere, too.

> Madelyn, nine years old, daughter of Cindy McCormick
> Martinusen, author of *Winter Passing*

I think Lucy and Serena are really cool. I can't wait to read the next HIDDEN DIARY book.

> Bethany, nine years old, daughter of Janet Holm McHenry,
> author of *PrayerWalk* & *Girlfriend Gatherings*

Books by
Sandra Byrd
FROM BETHANY HOUSE PUBLISHERS

Girl Talk

THE HIDDEN DIARY
Cross My Heart
Make a Wish
Just Between Friends
Take a Bow

THE
HIDDEN
DIARY

Cross My Heart

SANDRA BYRD

BETHANY HOUSE
MINNEAPOLIS, MINNESOTA

Published by Bethany House Publishers
A Ministry of Bethany Fellowship International
11400 Hampshire Avenue South
Bloomington, Minnesota 55438
www.bethanyhouse.com

Printed in the United States of America by
Bethany Press International, Bloomington, Minnesota 55438

Library of Congress Cataloging-in-Publication Data

Byrd, Sandra.
    Cross my heart / by Sandra Byrd.
       p.   cm. — (The hidden diary ; bk. 1)
Summary: While on Catalina Island for the summer, Lucy, who is about to be twelve, discovers a mysterious diary from 1932 and rediscovers Christ, both of which help her overcome her feelings of not belonging.
    ISBN 0-7642-2480-8 (pbk.)
    [1. Diaries—Fiction. 2. Friendship—Fiction. 3. Christian life—Fiction. 4. Santa Catalina Island (Calif.)—Fiction.] I. Title.
    PZ7.B9898 Cr   2001
    [Fic]—dc21   2001001257

For my husband, Michael.

A man of His word.

Contents

Beach Dreams

Saturday afternoon . . .

Lucy Larson lifted her sunglasses and peered at her arms. Hopeless. No tan, only pink. Always pink. *That's what strawberry blond means. My hair is reddish blond, so I should forget about getting a tan. I always end up looking like a strawberry!*

But that wouldn't ruin *this* summer. As soon as her cousin Katie joined her on Catalina Island, they would have a blast. Especially on Lucy's twelfth birthday, which was coming up in thirteen days.

A baby crab picked its way from the ocean toward Lucy's towel.

Seven-year-old Claudette Kingsley squealed. "Will it bite me?"

"No, Claudette. If you leave it alone, it will go away."

Claudette squeezed her eyes shut. "They're scary! Lots of sea creatures are scary. That's why I don't like to go swimming."

Mama mia. Every summer that Claudette's dad and

9

Lucy's dad worked together, Claudette found something new to be afraid of.

"I love to swim," Lucy said. "I'll come with you sometime so you won't be afraid. When Katie comes, we're going swimming every day. And we're going horseback riding—"

"Horses bite," Claudette interrupted.

"We're going to have a golf cart race. Go snorkeling."

"Snorkeling is dangerous."

Lucy smiled and shook her head at Claudette, then flipped through her magazine, deciding to take the quiz, "How to Choose a Best Friend." She'd answered one or two questions in her head before Claudette interrupted.

"Can I come on the golf carts?" Claudette asked. "Will you let me do things with you guys *every* day, even when you're not baby-sitting me?"

Lucy looked up and said, "We'll see." That's what her mother said when she didn't want to say no yet, even though she was going to say no sooner or later. Claudette's smile dropped.

"I'll definitely take you on a golf cart ride, okay?" Lucy said.

"Okay!" Claudette's smiled perked up. "I'm glad our dads are working together again this summer," she said. "I wonder where they are."

Lucy stared at the water off of the tiny southern California island of Catalina, which was twenty-three miles across the channel from Los Angeles. "Look for a rickety old tanker named the *Lickety Split*. That's what their research boat is called." Their dads, both professors studying plants, were beginning their summer research project this week.

A Koosh Ball skimmed the air and landed a few feet away from the two girls. From behind her sunglasses Lucy spied on a group of kids about her age calling out one another's names as they played. Two girls splashed in the surf together, screaming with laughter. Another noisy group tossed a volleyball. Suddenly Lucy felt left out.

She checked her watch. *Only twenty-one hours till Katie arrives.* Then *she'd* have a friend her own age here, too! Lucy glanced at the quiz once more before closing her magazine.

The Koosh Ball soared again, this time landing on Lucy's towel. She grabbed it and stood up. A girl about Lucy's age walked over, her long brown hair shimmering like the water.

"Here." Lucy handed it to her and smiled.

The girl smiled back and looked toward where her friends were hanging out. "Thanks," she said. "Would you like to—"

A girl in a pink T-shirt ran over, dropped her sunglasses into a nearby beach bag, and grabbed the dark-haired girl's arm. "Didn't your mother ever teach you not to talk to strangers?" She shot a cool glance at Lucy and flipped her ponytail as she dragged the friendly girl back to the others.

Lucy swallowed a big lump in her throat. This felt too much like last summer. And the summer before. *It's okay,* Lucy reminded herself. *Katie will be here soon.*

"Let's go," Lucy sighed. "Your mom wants you back in ten minutes." Lucy slid her feet into her flower-power sandals and stuffed her towel into the beach basket. She stopped for a minute, watching as the little sand crab made its way toward the spot where the noisy girls sat. Finally the crab clawed its way up into the mean girl's beach bag.

"I guess crabs hang out in pairs," Lucy whispered to

herself as she stepped onto the pavement. A few minutes later they arrived at Claudette's house. "Here you are." Lucy reached into her pocket and felt the two five-dollar bills Claudette's mom had paid Lucy in advance.

Claudette ran into her house. "Bye!" she called out.

Lucy waved back and smiled at Claudette before heading to her own house.

Well, it wasn't a house, really. More like a cottage. But a cottage was okay. It had everything they needed for an awesome summer. Even a piano.

Twenty and a half hours till Katie comes! Yahoo!

Lucy shut the creaking screen door behind her and stepped inside to get something to drink. "I'm home!" she called as she entered the kitchen.

The fridge was nearly empty—no time to shop for much yet. Lucy found a can of Dr Pepper and popped open the top. Her mother walked into the room, her blond hair pulled back, a thin film of sweat glazing her forehead.

"What's for dinner?" Lucy asked. Then she noticed the worry lines creasing her mom's face. "What's the matter?"

Her mother stared out the kitchen window.

Lucy, following her mother's glance, noticed several boats off the coast. *Dad's out on the boat*, she thought with a jolt. *Is it old and dangerous after all?* "Is Dad okay?"

"Dad's fine." Her mother took Lucy's hand in her own.

Lucy glanced up, alarmed. They hardly ever held hands anymore.

"But I do have bad news."

Oh No!

Saturday afternoon and evening . . .

"What bad news, Mom?"

"It's about Katie."

"Oh no! What happened? Is she hurt?"

"No," her mother said. "Katie's okay. But Aunt Cathy slipped on some tiles while watering the garden and broke her leg in several places. She's in the hospital, and she'll be in a wheelchair for most of the summer."

"Oh, Mom! That's *awful*! But Grammy and Gramps will be able to help her out, right?"

"Right. There's more." She looked Lucy straight in the eyes. "Katie has to help her mother, too. She has to stay home and help Aunt Cathy."

"It's all right, Mom. I can find something to do for a week or two. When can she come?"

"She's not coming," Mom said.

"Not at all?"

"Not at all. Aunt Cathy won't be able to walk for

months, and she's going to need Katie's help. I'm sorry, honey, but it could have been a lot worse. We have to be thankful that Aunt Cathy's okay."

"I *am* thankful," Lucy said. She sank back into the wicker chair. "But what in the world am I going to do here all summer? You guys will be out scouting plants or seaweed all day." She stared at her mother's easel. "Or painting."

"You could go with us to find plants."

"Mom, I've done this every summer. Remember last year? Fern fronds in Alaska?"

"The scenery was beautiful," Mom reminded her.

"If you're a moose. Or a painter. To me it's boring. I know Dad has to do these research things in the summer, but . . ." Her voice trailed off. Lucy stared at her hands. "Katie and I had big plans. Now I'll be alone."

"You won't be alone," her mom said. "Claudette will be here."

Lucy rolled her eyes. "No offense, Mom, but Claudette's idea of an adventure is putting hot sauce on her taco. She's a nice kid, but she's little. She's afraid of old houses. She's too young to ride horses or snorkel."

Lucy chewed on her thumbnail, thinking. Maybe she could fly back home and stay with her cousin. If she hurried, she could still sign up for tennis camp. The summer would be saved!

"What if I go home and stay with Katie, to help Aunt Cathy?" Lucy offered. "They could probably use the help."

Her mother sank into her chair cushion. "You mean you'd rather do that? Dad and I thought this could be a new beginning for us as a family. You know, a fresh start after these last few difficult years."

Lucy didn't even want to think about her family's past few difficult years.

"Mom, you know I love you and Dad." Lucy squeezed her mother's hand. "But I want one summer like a normal kid. Just one, doing normal stuff with other kids my same age. That's all I'm asking. And you promised that to me this year."

She looked at her still-silent mother. "Remember last summer? There were four kids in town, and they were all totally rude. Not one of them was nice. They called me names. Remember?"

Her mother quietly withdrew her hand. "I remember. And Dad and I did promise you a normal summer with Katie this year. I'll talk about it with Dad after dinner. Speaking of which, let's head down the street to Vons and buy groceries."

Lucy winced at the sadness in her mother's eyes. But a girl could only take so many of these solo science trips. *It really is best if I go back home. I know they'll understand once they think about it.*

She slipped her flower-powers back on and hoped her dad would see it her way.

☂ ☂ ☂

Later, after dinner, Lucy lugged a box up the stairs. It had just been delivered and was addressed to her. Even though she was excited to open it, her hands grew unsteady.

She had other things on her mind.

Her parents were talking about her. *Deciding.* Lucy sat down in the middle of the floor and snapped open her Swiss army knife. After sliding the blade under the tape, Lucy neatly slit open the sides.

What if they say I have to stay? Another summer by myself? She lifted each flap of the box carefully and took out a stack of T-shirts and shorts she had left at Grammy's. Tucked safely inside the nest of clothing was a large wrapped gift. Lucy ran her fingers along the edges and started to unwrap it.

Just then she heard a knock on the door.

"Lucy?" her father asked. "Can we come in?"

"Sure." Lucy left the gift wedged between the clothes and settled onto one of the twin beds as her parents stepped into the room. Her breath came faster as she looked into her parents' faces, trying to guess what they were thinking.

Her dad scratched his beard thoughtfully, and then the two of them sat down together on the other bed.

"We've given this both thought and prayer," her dad started.

Oh yeah, Lucy thought. *I forgot they pray now.* She wasn't used to that. It was nice, in a different sort of way.

Dad continued. "We understand how hard it must be for you to be with adults all the time—"

"No, Dad," Lucy interrupted. "I like being with you guys. It's just . . . well, you know. I don't know any kids my own age here. I want to do normal things for just one summer. Swimming. Parties. Horseback riding. Shopping. I don't really want to pick weeds again."

"Weeds? These aren't weeds." Dad got that university professor glaze in his eyes. "They're potentially endangered indigenous fauna that—"

Lucy's mother gently laid her hand on his arm, and her father stopped talking. Mom continued, "We know how much you want to be with friends. So if you'd like, we'll call Grammy and Gramps and ask if you could please spend the summer with them. They know you are thinking about it. Then you'll get to be right near Katie."

She thought she'd feel relief, but instead a knot of worry bunched up under Lucy's ribs. Now that she thought about it, twelve weeks away from Mom and Dad was a long time. Even if she was at Grammy's house. On the other hand, twelve weeks of boredom was a long time, too. What should she do?

No snorkeling this summer, she reminded herself. *No horses, no camping—*

"Or," Dad interrupted her thoughts, "if you want to stay here, I'll scale back work. Your mom and I made a commitment to spend more time together as a family. Camping, snorkeling. Of course you can learn to kayak. I promised I'd teach you."

Lucy smiled. "A bribe." Her father knew how much she loved boating.

"We hope you'll stay," Mom said.

"The decision is yours. And you don't have to make it right away." Dad walked over to Lucy and planted a kiss on her forehead. "I told Grammy we'd call her on Friday night and let her know what we're going to do. Let's think it over and not rush a decision this time, okay?"

"All right." Lucy rolled her eyes. Why did everyone always think she rushed decisions? As she crossed her arms over her chest, she felt some leftover sunscreen grease. "I'd better take a shower."

Her mom stepped into the hallway and took a towel from the linen closet, then lightly tossed it onto Lucy's bed. "We'll be downstairs, okay?" Dad gently shut the door behind him.

Now what? If she chose to go, she'd hurt their feelings and not be working toward building their family back together again. But what if she stayed, and they got caught up in their work like they'd always done before, forgetting about their promise to spend time together? She'd be stuck plucking plants all summer or baby-sitting Claudette.

Lucy had to admit she felt much happier around her parents now, since they'd been going to church. She fearfully allowed a thought in. *But what if all this religious stuff goes away and Mom and Dad don't get along again?*

Lucy knelt next to the half-opened box. She cautiously opened the army knife again and slit the tape on the sides of the gift wrapping. Out slid a large diary. Taped to the front was a card.

> *Have a wonderful summer. Be sure to write down your island adventures! Love, Grammy.*

Lucy placed the unopened diary on the night table next to the still-shrink-wrapped Bible from her parents. *There might not be many island adventures.* Lucy glanced around the room and at the empty bed that would have been Katie's. No sneaking in midnight snacks. No giggle fits. No shopping for treasures together.

But maybe we can *do all those things—just not on Catalina. At Grammy's house or Katie's house instead.*

Lucy's chest ached as she thought of telling her parents. She pictured their hopeful eyes a few minutes before. *I'll come back to visit,* she decided.

Lucy started down the stairs to tell them her decision. She stopped on the third step.

If I tell them now, they'll think I'm rushing my decision, even though I'm not. I'll just get my pajamas on and read.

First, her shower. She twisted off her rings, not wanting to lose the new turquoise ring, which was loose. After a yank, she slipped the mood ring off of her left hand, too.

Lucy reached for a tiny drawer in the built-in dresser in the back of the closet. It was the only drawer left empty after unpacking, and she wanted a special home for her rings. She tugged on the drawer, but nothing happened.

Lucy wriggled the slender blade of her army knife into a crack on the side. Victory! The drawer finally gave way as she jerked and pried. One last wriggle and the drawer squeaked free. Paint chips and a small chunk of wood fell onto the floor.

Oh no! Did I break it? She picked up the piece of wood and tried to shove it back into place. When she peered inside the hole, however, she saw something else.

She opened the drawer all the way. Her breath came fast as she spied a tiny compartment. The drawer had a false back!

Lucy's hand shook as she reached into the compartment and pulled out a folded, yellowed letter and a small tarnished key.

The Mystery

Saturday night . . .

Lucy balanced the letter and the key in her open palm, slowly breathing out without taking her eyes off of her find. She could see the ink through the fragile paper even though the letter was folded in thirds. A light crust coated the inside of the key; she scraped it off with her fingernail. Lucy kept her palm flat and walked over to her dresser, placing the letter on top of it. As she set the letter down, a puff of stale air rose from it—a smell like dust, mold, and perfume. She set the key down beside it, then perched on the edge of her bed, staring at them.

Should I read it? It belonged to someone else, even if she didn't know to whom. Lucy's parents had always taught her to respect the privacy of the owners of the homes they stayed in during their summer research trips.

Glancing at the towel, Lucy remembered her shower. Maybe a few minutes in the shower would clear things up, give her an idea of what she should do next. After tossing her rings into the drawer she'd found, she worked it shut again. Grabbing the towel, she headed into the shower.

The water came out in cold spurts, then a blast of hot that peeled her skin. She scrubbed away the film of sunscreen and rinsed away the sand still clinging between her toes.

Mama mia! How long has it been since someone opened that drawer, anyway?

Afterward, Lucy rubbed some lotion over her legs. *Too short. Katie's legs are long and thin, like a grasshopper's.* Lucy stared at her teeth in the mirror. She wasn't done eating yet. No use brushing them at this point.

After tossing the towel over the glass doorknob, she slipped into her pajamas and glanced at the letter.

This house didn't really belong to a person, not like some of the other summers when people rented out their houses to Lucy's family. This house belonged to the university.

After punching her pillow into shape, Lucy stepped back to the dresser to grab her Amelia Earhart book. Her fingers gripped the spine of the book, but her eyes lingered on the letter, then wandered to the key. Was it really the same as someone's personal mail?

She hopped into bed, trying to keep her mind on Amelia's amazing first flight across the Atlantic. Forcing her eyes to concentrate on each and every word wasn't working, so Lucy tried reading ahead, seeing if she could skip to the good parts. *Yesterday, they all seemed like good parts. Why doesn't it feel that way today?*

A snack, yeah, that was it. She needed a snack. She

folded the book upside down over Tender Teddy and grabbed her plastic Jelly Belly container from underneath the bed. Jelly Bellies made anything better! After opening the case, she surveyed her choices. Juicy Pear. Bubble Gum. Buttered Popcorn. Island Punch. Of course! Here on an island, Island Punch was the best choice. Lucy tossed a few into her mouth and perched on the edge of her bed, again staring at the letter and key. The snack hadn't settled her at all.

This house didn't belong to anyone, really, Lucy decided. So she wouldn't be doing anything wrong to read the letter. And anyway, if the writer didn't want anyone to read the letter, why would she have left it there? Maybe there was someone who needed help, and if Lucy didn't read the letter, she wouldn't be able to help. It wouldn't be nice. She'd do the right thing. She'd read the letter and offer help if someone needed it.

Lucy closed the book, set Tender Teddy on her pillow, and walked toward the letter. Next, she ran her hands over her pajama pants to make sure they didn't have any candy goo on them that might leave a stain. She touched the letter and gently grasped it between finger and thumb. With the other hand she took the key.

Breaths came faster; her head got airy and her teeth icy all at once. As soon as she held both letter and key, she sat cross-legged on the cool floor, feeling the smooth wood beneath her cotton pajamas. The key balanced on her knee. Barely.

First, she unfolded one section of the letter and then the other. The ink had probably been deep black at one time, but now it had faded to pale gray. The handwriting was scratchy. It looked like two different kinds of handwriting, one with curlicues and one with more block-style writing. Two people, maybe. Lucy read the date on top—1932.

Wow! Before Mom and Dad were born, way before that. And one of Amelia Earhart's best years, too!

The letter began,

Dearest Reader,

Reader! That meant whoever was reading it, not anyone in particular! Lucy's breathing still sped along. Her hungry eyes ate up the words on the page, not skipping or skimming anything as she read.

Serena and I had a swell summer, the best ever, really, for the best of friends. Everything was nifty, from the party that started it all to the one that we're going to tonight, I hope! It should be the cat's meow! And we wrote it all down in our diary—every experience, each hope, some dangerous things, and of course every disagreement (well, just a few) for posterity. But we couldn't decide which of us got to take the diary home at the end of the summer.

Lucy smiled. *"Cat's meow."* Definitely old-timey.
The handwriting changed to the block style.

mary's reading Agatha Christie mystery novels, and

we thought how nifty it would be to create a mystery of our own! So, dear reader, we hid the diary right here on the Island, somewhere we spend a lot of time, saving our secrets in high places. We wanted to leave a bit of mystery of our own to end the summer.

Lucy's eyes followed the words as they turned back into the curlicue style.

To make things interesting, one of us kept the diary at her house, and one of us kept the key, with this letter. If no one's found the diary before you find this letter, it should be waiting for you. You can walk all over our words, but no one will ever know. We wrote it together, every word. We hope it stays hidden for a good long time (and safe from Joey, who needs to mind his own potatoes).

Now the handwriting changed back to the other writer again.

Except you, dear reader, if you can find it. But if you find the diary, please keep it to yourself. Don't show it around, like Joey—that old gumdrop—wants to. Diaries are private. Good luck.

Faithful Friends,
Mary and Serena

Lucy ran her trembling fingertip across the key. A diary key. It opened a hidden diary, full of secrets. What could be in there? What did those girls do—what adventures did they have? What kind of dangerous things? What kind of disagreements? Lucy's heart pumped two beats every second instead of one. Where could that diary be hidden? She had to find it. She would.

Snatching the letter from her lap, she hopped up and ran down the stairs.

"Mom! Dad! A mystery!"

Dad looked up from the books and papers he'd spread across the kitchen table. Mom kept staring at the easel she was painting upon.

Lucy rolled her eyes. Would her mom *ever* stop paying so much attention to her work or her cleaning or *whatever* that she couldn't hear what anyone else was saying?

"Mom!" she said. This time her mother looked up.

"What is it, Sparky?" her dad asked.

Lucy waved the paper and key in front of them, coming to a slippery stop as her socks glided across the tile.

She pulled up a chair next to her dad and watched to see what her mother would do. Her mom actually set down her brushes and sat down next to Lucy.

"Guess what I found? And guess what I'm *going* to find!"

Spilling the words out, she explained how she'd found the letter and the key in a tiny drawer stuck shut by humidity and time, and how she'd struggled with whether she should read it.

"Did I do the right thing?"

Her dad tousled her hair. "Yes, of course. This house isn't a private residence like the others. And the writers even said they meant for someone to find it, right?"

"Right!" Lucy smiled. "Now I need to find the diary!"

Her mom and dad glanced at each other.

"What?" Lucy asked. "They said they meant for me to find the diary, too!"

A full minute must have ticked by, and Lucy heard the meowing of the neighbor's cat outside.

"Yes, but it will be hard to know what house it's located in. And who knows who lives there now? Maybe the diary has already been found. Or maybe the writer changed her mind and took the diary out of hiding the next summer."

"She said they *wanted* to make a mystery! They wouldn't ruin it!" Lucy's hopes started to drop like pebbles tossed overboard that slowly settle into the sand. "And, uh, we can find the house."

Lucy didn't feel so confident now. *How? Where? We don't even know anyone here. Remember? That's why you want to stay with Grammy this summer.* She didn't know anyone, and nothing good was going to happen. Lucy let the paper drift onto the table by her dad's papers.

"I have an idea," her mother said. She reached over and opened the Catalina Island Directory next to the phone. After thumbing through a few pages, she smiled. "Aha!"

Lucy looked into her mother's eyes. "What is it?"

"The Catalina Island Historical Society." She tapped the page. "See? And it's open tomorrow. How about if you and I go to lunch tomorrow, and afterward we stop by. Maybe they can tell us who lived in this house in 1932.

Perhaps we can trace it that way."

"Would you really, Mom?" Lucy put her arms around her mother for a second before she dropped them to her sides. "I know how busy you are with work right now." Lucy glanced at the canvas. "If you take me there, I prom- ise I'll ask all the questions and everything and it won't take long."

Her mother's eyes softened. "I always have time for you."

Lucy's nose wrinkled. Well, this was new. But who was she to question her mother's changed attitude if it was going to lead to finding the hidden diary?

Octopus Salad

Late Sunday morning . . .

The next morning, Lucy awoke to a light knock on her door.

"Lucy?"

"Yeah, Dad?" She sat up, leaned over, and grabbed her bear, which had fallen off the bed during the night. Then she pushed her hair behind her ears.

Her dad opened her door and stepped into her room with a tray of toast and orange juice. "Your mom and I are going to have a Bible study downstairs since we haven't found a church for the summer yet. Would you like to join us in a couple of minutes?"

So they planned to keep going to church, even here. They must be serious. Lucy glanced over at her unwrapped Bible. "I don't think so," she said. "I'm going to clean up and get ready to go to lunch with Mom. Okay?"

Her dad said nothing, but it looked like the corners of his mouth drooped, even though his beard hid them. "All right." He set the tray down. "I think Mom will want to get going about noon. You guys can eat and visit the historical society. But you'll need to get back to help me prepare dinner. Claudette and her family are coming over to eat tonight."

He closed the door.

Lucy got up and opened her window, letting in the sea breeze. It carried in the light perfume of white jasmine blooming like soft white stars on the backyard bushes. After finishing her toast and juice, she heard the low rumble of her parents' voices filtering up through the floor vents and felt strangely guilty that she wasn't down there with them.

But how do I know this whole church thing will even last? It didn't last time. Last time Lucy was the one who wanted to keep going to Sunday school, who kept asking if they could please go to church, begging to sing in the Easter concert. But her parents were always too busy, and slowly, they stopped going at all. So Lucy had stopped going, too. It seemed like they'd forgotten all about it. Till last spring.

When she put her ear against the floor vents, Lucy clearly heard her father and mother. Her dad read a piece out of the Bible, and then they did something strange. They sang a worship song. Just the two of them, without any music. Her mom said "Amen" in a voice gentler than Lucy remembered hearing.

Peace drifted over Lucy like the breeze from the window; she closed her eyes and was carried away to somewhere else, somewhere as sweet as the jasmine. Her lips opened, and she whispered her own song.

"Jesus loves me, this I know,

For the Bible tells me so."

Lucy's eyes flew open. She hadn't even realized she remembered any songs about Jesus.

Well. Her face flushed. She stood up and made her bed. *I'd better get dressed. I want to be ready when Mom wants to go,* she told herself as she pulled the sheets up and tried to smooth the bedspread. She pulled on cutoff shorts and a Hawaiian T-shirt, then retrieved her rings. The drawer still stuck, but it opened when she tugged twice.

Her mood ring turned green. Green meant thoughtful.

After tidying up her room, Lucy thought about emailing her cousin Katie. What would she say, though? Surely Grammy would have told Katie that Lucy might come home, and Katie would ask Lucy what she was going to do. *Then* what would Lucy say? She had no answer for that yet. Instead, Lucy sat down and read the old letter again.

A bit later her mom knocked on the door.

"Ready?" she asked as she set a small load of clean clothes on Lucy's bed.

"Yes!" Lucy said. "I'll be down in a minute!"

She took the key and letter and tucked them safely into the large pocket of her canvas shoulder bag. She grabbed a couple of dollars and stuffed them in, too, just in case. She clipped her hair back with some gray-green clips that matched her eye color and stood on her tippy-toes, trying to see more of herself in the dresser's mirror. Then she ran downstairs.

"Where do you want to go?" her mom asked as they walked the few short blocks to the main shopping and eating area of town. Avalon was only two miles square, and most businesses and restaurants were only a few blocks away from their house, so it was a quick walk to anywhere.

"Somewhere . . . fun. Different," Lucy answered.

"How about King's Fish Market?" her mother suggested. Lucy nodded her agreement, and they soon settled into two plastic chairs on a pier overlooking the water.

A young waitress came to take their order.

"I'll have fish and chips," Lucy's mother ordered. "And an iced tea, please."

Lucy snapped her menu shut. "Octopus salad," she announced. "And a Dr Pepper."

"Are you sure?" The waitress's eyes opened wide and she stood by the table, as if waiting for a changed order.

"I'm sure." Lucy smiled and handed her menu over.

Her mother waited till the waitress left before giggling.

Lucy giggled back. They hadn't giggled together for quite a while. "Might as well try something new, ya know. It's not every day octopus salad is on the menu."

"You can order it all summer if you like," her mother said.

An electric feeling passed between them, and the conversation stopped. Lucy had better remind her mom that she didn't know where she was spending the whole summer. "I haven't decided if I'm staying or not, remember?" she said softly.

"Oh yes, I . . . I remember," her mother said. "Go ahead and take the whole week to decide, like Dad said."

"Thanks for taking me today, Mom," Lucy changed the subject. "It means a lot to me. It's fun!"

"Me too," her mom said. "It will be fun to see if the historical society can help us."

Lucy smiled. "That's what they're there for, right?"

🐜 🐜 🐜

After lunch, Lucy and her mom walked along the beach on the way to the historical society. Kids swarmed all over the beach and even raced each other in the little dinghies from their parents' boats. A group of girls sat together listening to a low radio and chatting together, their heads bent close to one another as their bodies fanned out in the sand like petals on a flower.

"I think it's right across the street," Lucy's mom said, waiting as several golf carts passed by. There were almost no cars on the Island; most people got around in golf carts. Lucy forced her gaze away from the girls and toward the place her mother pointed to. It was a small space underneath a much larger ivory-capped building that also housed the famous ballroom and movie theater.

"Hello, may I help you?" A tanned, wrinkled, grandmotherly woman grinned as they entered.

Lucy stepped forward and took the letter from her shoulder bag. "Yes, I'm, uh, hoping you can help me with a little research. We're staying at 234 Pebble Road. I'm wondering if you have some record of who might have lived there in 1932. I know it's an awfully long time ago, but, well . . ."

The old lady nodded, then turned her back to them. The flesh on her ample upper arms shook as she took down a sturdy leather book from a shelf. Finally she turned toward them and spoke.

"It looks like 234 Pebble Road was sold in 1934 to the university." She looked up at Lucy's mother. "Are you with the university?"

"My husband is affiliated with a sister college," she answered.

"I'm sorry," the woman said. "We know it was sold, but no further information. You might be able to leave the Island and go over town on the mainland to check the property records, but they didn't keep a lot of information back then like they do now." She turned her back to them again and jostled the leather book back onto its shelf.

Lucy's world melted beneath her. Somehow she remembered her manners.

"Thank you," she mumbled. As she folded the letter, she said to her mother, "I guess I'll never find out about Mary and Serena," she said.

The old woman turned around and crinkled her eyes at Lucy. "Did you say Serena?"

Crabby Points the Way

Sunday afternoon and evening . . .

Lucy dug the letter out of her shoulder bag again, just to make sure she got the name right.

"Yes, yes, it's really Serena," she said, scanning the letter again.

"Well, now." The old lady drew up her chair behind the counter, her cloudy eyes seeming to focus a bit.

"My mama ran around with a few girls on the Island when she was coming up. One of them I've heard her talk of was named Serena." She looked pointedly at Lucy and her mother. "This is a small island, you realize. Only a handful more than three thousand people live here now, 'bout the same as in those days. Everybody knows everybody else. Not too many people named Serena."

Lucy said nothing, waiting on the woman.

"My mama passed on many years ago."

Great. Another dead end. Lucy folded the letter up yet again and stuffed it back into her shoulder bag.

The old lady had a shine in her eyes. "Now, young Serena, she's a different story."

"Young Serena?" Both Lucy and her mother said it at the same time.

"Related somehow to the old Serena, I'm sure. Strange name, as I said. Great-granddaughter, I think. Or maybe great-niece. I'm not sure. But she's still here."

"Do you know where she lives?" Lucy jumped in.

"Indeed I do." She dug out a street map, fumbling with it. "Used to work at parcel delivery service. Know where just about everyone lives." A few seconds ticked by. Her face got pink. "Well, I did know." She looked apologetic. "Guess I'm not sure of the house number." She tapped her head with a finger. "Getting old, you know." Her gnarled fingers gripped a pen and scribbled something down. "This is the street, and the street's not all that long. Sorry I can't do better."

She handed a torn scrap of paper to Lucy's mother.

"Marine Way," her mother read aloud.

"Thank you!" Lucy said as they headed out into the bright sunshine.

"Mom, can we go find the street right now?" Lucy pulled her straw hat down to shade her eyes. Maybe someone would be outside and they could ask where Serena lived!

Her mother checked her watch. "Hmm. I don't think so. We need to walk all the way over to Vons, buy the few extras Dad wanted, and get home in enough time to help him with dinner before the Kingsleys come."

"Mo-om!" Lucy wailed. "Please! This is important."

Her mother smiled. "It is. But after all, the diary has waited all these years. I think it can wait a couple more hours."

Lucy heaved a sigh.

"You know Dad likes to take a walk after dinner to help digest his food," her mother continued. "Maybe if the Kingsleys don't stay too late, we can go for an after-dinner stroll and see how many houses are on Marine Way."

"Okay." It wasn't perfect, but it was the best Lucy was going to get.

❦ ❦ ❦

"Like my hair clips?" Claudette scooted her chair next to Lucy's in the tiny dining alcove off of the kitchen. If Claudette got any closer, Lucy wouldn't be able to lift her elbows to use a knife.

Lucy glanced at the sunflower clips in Claudette's hair. "Of course I like them, Claudette. They're just like a pair of mine!"

"I know. I thought we could be twins!" Claudette said. "I brought you a present." She dug into her pocket and found a chunk of bubble gum. It was still in its wrapper but had attracted a lot of pocket lint.

"It's cotton candy flavored. Can I have some of your Jelly Bellies?"

"Maybe later, kiddo." Lucy hid the gum under the side of her plate.

"I want to get you another present, but it's at the store. I want us to buy it together. Can you take me shopping tomorrow?"

Lucy looked through the archway into the kitchen. Her mother must have overheard. She tapped the calendar on the fridge. "You agreed to baby-sit her tomorrow morning and once more this week."

"Okay, I'll take you tomorrow morning. Just for a few minutes, though."

Man alive. Six o'clock and we haven't even eaten yet. Lucy kept watching her dad's face for circles under his eyes, a yawn, anything that showed he was tired. So far so good, and it was time to get the chow on the table.

"Here's the food!" Dad announced as he stepped in from the kitchen. Lucy's mom and Mrs. Kingsley followed him.

"Smells great, Nathan," Mr. Kingsley said.

Soon everyone sat at the table.

"Would you like to pray?" Lucy's dad asked Mr. Kingsley.

"No, Nathan, go right ahead. A man in his own house, and all," Mr. Kingsley answered.

Lucy's dad cleared his throat. For once he seemed uncomfortable talking.

"Let's bow our heads, shall we?"

Lucy closed her eyes.

"Uh, Lord, thank you for the food and for our friends and for the work we have before us this summer. Thank you for always being with us, even when we can't sense you near. Amen."

Lucy opened her eyes. Yum, the smell of almond rice drifted down the table, mixing with the honey-ginger glaze on the chicken. Lucy drank in the smell. Her dad was the best cook in the world.

After dinner, Lucy's mom pushed away from the table first. "I'll clean up since you did the cooking, Nathan." She stacked a few plates on top of one another.

"I'll help," Mrs. Kingsley said. She grabbed a handful of silverware, which clinked and clanked against one another. "You two can have some time together."

People didn't seem to realize Claudette was almost five years younger than she! Lucy rolled her eyes. But Claudette looked up at her with the sweetest smile. Even Lucy wanted to smile back.

"Come on, I'll bet you have a new jump rope song to show me," Lucy said, heading upstairs. "And I'll give you some Jelly Bellies."

Less than an hour later, they were saying good-bye at the door. Lucy closed it behind them as quickly as she could without seeming rude.

"So, Dad, up for a little walk?"

"Oh dear," he said. "I am sooooo tired. I think I might call it an early night." He plopped down in his chair, the air hissing out of the cushion as it absorbed his full weight.

Panic froze Lucy's heart.

"I've got work to do," her mother said, turning her back. "Lots of it." She headed toward her easel.

Mama mia. Then Lucy heard a tiny laugh from behind

38

the pillow Dad held over his face.

"You guys are teasing me!"

Mom turned from her easel and smiled. "Yes." Her dad burst out laughing.

Lucy whipped out the scrap the old lady had written the address on. "Good. Because *guess what?* That street is right behind ours!"

"Makes sense," Dad said as he stroked his beard. "Can't have been that many streets built back then. Had to be close."

"It's close, all right." Lucy slid her feet into her flower-powers, and the three of them headed out the door.

They walked down the block; though it was early evening, it grew dusky dark, the mountains behind them shading the sun as it dipped toward the Pacific Ocean. Orange trees bowed low, their branches struggling with the weight of fruit. A couple of people enjoying the cool of the evening nodded hello as they passed by. A few houses later Lucy's family turned onto Marine Way.

Which house could it be? They all looked old and expensive.

Lucy's dad stopped to look at a bush. A bunch of boys stared at him as he examined the leaves.

Not again! Another plant moment.

"Come on, Dad!" She tugged on his arm to hurry down the road.

Three or four houses down, on the side that backed to Lucy's street, a group of girls sat on a porch.

Fear and thrill raced through Lucy's veins, competing for her attention.

"Maybe that's it," her mother whispered. Lucy said nothing, nodding.

"Why don't you go ask?" Her dad nudged her.

Lucy said nothing.

They were almost in front of the house now. Someone called out, "Julie, your mom is on the phone."

A thin girl stood up and grabbed the cordless phone. Lucy held her breath. The crabby girl from the beach!

"Serena, heads up."

Serena! Lucy and her mother looked at each other.

A teenaged boy leaned out the front door and tossed a can of pop to a girl with shiny, dark brown hair. Lucy's heart caught a beat. The nice girl from the beach!

"Do you want to go and talk with them?" Dad asked. "We can go with you."

"Um, no thanks." Not with that crabby girl there. Lucy kept walking, her head down. What a disappointment!

But I'll be back in the morning, she promised herself. *With the letter and the key.*

Saludad, Amigos

Monday morning . . .

Today was the day! Lucy was up making toast before her dad had even left for work.

"Hey! What are you doing up so early? Coming out with me to pick weeds?" he teased.

"Um, no," Lucy said. "You know why I'm up!" She peeled the crust off of her toast but didn't take more than one bite. Her stomach felt queasy all of a sudden. Too many Jelly Bellies. Or something else.

"I know, you're eager to go over to Serena's house. Make sure you take your two-way radio. And don't go inside their house," Dad warned. "They're still strangers."

"Oh, Dad." Lucy rolled the crust into a gooey ball.

"But first," Mom said as she poured another cup of coffee, "you've got shopping to do."

"WHAT?" Lucy dropped the crust ball onto the table.

"You're baby-sitting, remember? And didn't you promise to take Claudette shopping this morning?"

Lucy slapped her forehead. "How about if I go over to Serena's first?" She ran and looked into the hallway mirror. Messy hair, two minutes to fix. Clothes, no problem. She could be ready to go anytime.

Dad stood up and headed out to their golf cart. "I'll see you two later." He kissed them both before heading out the door.

"So, Mom, whadd'ya say?"

"Lucy, it's rude to go to someone's house before ten in the morning. Someone you don't even know," Mom said.

Lucy's face pinched up. Mom could be so unrealistic. But after all, Lucy *had* promised to baby-sit.

🌴 🌴 🌴

Lucy tried to be cheerful on the job, and a few hours later Claudette dragged Lucy down the street and into a gift shop on the main road. It was named Dove Books and Gifts, and the display windows were lined with Catalina seashells, sea horse stickers, books, and Bibles.

"What is this?"

"It's a Christian bookstore," Claudette answered. "Haven't you ever been in a Christian bookstore?"

"I'm not sure," Lucy said. "I don't remember."

"Come on." Claudette ran toward the back, reaching up to a rack where lots of trinkets sat together in plastic beach buckets. Claudette reached her hand into one bucket. "Close your eyes!"

"Claudette, why am I closing my eyes? You wanted me to come with you!"

"I want it to be a surprise."

Lucy closed her eyes.

Claudette stuffed whatever she had fished out of the buckets under her armpit and led the way to the cashier.

"Turn around so you can't peek," she ordered Lucy.

Claudette paid and grabbed Lucy's hand as they raced back toward the house. The sun warmed the pebbled roads as the sound of boat horns wailed in the distance.

"Listen to my new jump rope song," Claudette said. " 'Bubble gum, bubble gum, in a dish, how many pieces do you wish?' " Then she jumped up and down a bit, even though she didn't have a jump rope.

Lucy tousled Claudette's hair. "Cool song, kiddo. But it's time to take you home." *And I need to get to Serena's,* Lucy thought.

"But I want to give you your present at your house. In your room."

"All right. But then I need to take you back. Your mom will be expecting us."

As soon as they arrived at Lucy's house, Claudette called out a greeting to Lucy's mom and ran up the stairs.

Lucy followed. She popped open her Jelly Belly case, selected a Coconut and a Crushed Pineapple, and ate them together.

Claudette watched her, then unfolded the top crease of her blue paper shopping bag. She drew out two glow-in-the-dark crosses. "See? Aren't they cool? I want us to have matching crosses."

Ever since Claudette's parents had invited Lucy's parents back into a church, encouraging them to turn toward

Jesus again, Claudette thought it was her job to teach Lucy. Claudette watched Lucy's face closely. "Don't you like it?" she asked, her voice wavering.

"I do," Lucy said. She didn't know what else to say. She'd never had a cross in her room before.

"Are you a Christian?" Claudette asked.

"I, um, I am," Lucy said. "I think."

"I mean, if you asked Jesus to be your Savior forever and always including today, and if you told Him you sinned and you were sorry and you want to be friends with Him always, then you are," Claudette said in one giant breath.

Lucy'd probably been about Claudette's age when she first heard about Jesus at family camp. She had decided to follow Jesus then, forever and ever. She had wanted to be His friend. She just hadn't known what to do next when her family stopped going to church and her parents never talked about God anymore.

Actually, she reminded herself, *I think I was eight years old then*. In some ways it seemed long ago. In other ways, not too long at all.

"Can I have some Jelly Bellies?" Claudette pointed to the plastic case, and Lucy snapped it open for her, letting her choose what she liked.

Claudette chose a Coconut and a Crushed Pineapple and popped them into her mouth. Then she walked over to Lucy's mirror, peeled the sticky paper off of the glow-in-the-dark cross, and stuck it halfway up the mirror on the left-hand side. "For when you're scared at night," she said.

Claudette went downstairs, and Lucy grabbed her

shoulder bag with the letter and the key. *I hope Serena is home and will be easy to talk to.*

On her way out, Lucy stared at the cross. "For when you're scared," she whispered to herself. She went downstairs.

"I'm going, Mom."

"Got the two-way radio?"

"Yep," Lucy said. "Be back soon." She'd stared through her bedroom window and into her backyard the night before, noting that Serena's house was kitty-corner behind her own. Not too far!

Lucy took Claudette home, then walked up Marine Way and rounded the corner. Counting seven houses down, she got to Serena's.

Casa Romero, the wooden sign on the front door announced. *Saludad, Amigos.*

The Spanish she'd had the past two years was actually going to be useful. "Romero Home. Welcome, Friends."

Lucy knocked, softly at first, then more loudly. She waited another minute or two and knocked again. No one answered. She waited one whole minute, timing it by her watch. She knocked till her knuckles cracked. No answer.

She ran all the way home, not counting the houses this time.

When she got into the front room, she could barely keep back the tears of anger; when they unleashed, she flung them away with the back of her hand. A salty survivor trickled into the corner of her mouth.

"If only I hadn't baby-sat Claudette this morning, I could have talked to Serena."

She collapsed into the chair and tossed the shoulder bag, which slid along the tile floor.

Her mother finished two brushstrokes on her canvas. Then she looked straight at Lucy. "You'd promised Claudette. You had to keep the promise."

"I know!" Lucy stood up, angry, but not at her mother, although she was taking it out on her. She stomped up the stairs.

🐦 🐦 🐦

Later that night, after dinner, Lucy spoke up, more softly this time.

"Is it all right if I go over to Serena's again?"

Lucy's mother nodded. Lucy waited for her to mention her earlier temper tantrum; her mother said nothing.

Hmm. She pushed down a bad feeling and slipped into her flower-powers. As she trod up toward Marine Way, the mild sea breeze pushed her along. *Didn't even go to the beach today*, she thought with surprise. *I love the beach.*

Too busy pouting, her mother would have said. But Lucy wasn't her mother.

Seven houses down the next road, Lucy could barely bring herself to look, in case Crabby was on the porch again. She wasn't.

She drew herself up to the front door, just beneath the *Casa Romero* sign, and tapped on the door. This morning she had desperately wanted someone to answer; now she wasn't sure what to do if someone did.

"Hello?" a teenaged boy answered.

Lucy stared, the words glued to her throat like an apple in caramel.

"Uh, hello, my name is Lucy Larson. I live right there." She pointed to the house behind and kitty-corner to the one she was at.

Come on, Lucy, he doesn't care where you live! she thought. But she couldn't stop herself from pointing.

"Yes?" he said politely.

"I'm . . . I'm wondering if Serena is here." There. She'd said it.

"Yes, she is." He pointed to the porch swing. "Have a seat and I'll go get her."

The Second Serena

Monday night and Tuesday morning . . .

Lucy folded her hands in her lap to stop her trembling fingers. She could barely believe this was finally happening!

The screen door creaked, and Serena stepped out.

"Oh, hi," she said. She came over and sat on the porch swing next to Lucy. Lucy smiled. Serena might be popular, but she wasn't cliquish at all. Serena picked a fuzz ball off of her sweat shirt, her dark hair pulled back in a red-and-white-checked bandanna.

Lucy took in a deep breath. "I know this is going to seem weird, but . . . well, I found a letter and a diary key, and I think you might be interested."

Serena stopped picking fuzz. "Really?"

"Yeah." Lucy reached into her shoulder bag and pulled out the letter. "Read this. I found it in my house." She pointed past Serena's backyard, over toward her own cottage. "It was in my room, actually." She handed the letter to Serena, who looked puzzled but carefully opened and read the letter.

Lucy watched as Serena's face went from sea calm to open-eyed, then finally openmouthed amazement.

"Ay!" she exclaimed. "This Serena might have been my mother's grandma!"

Lucy stood up, her voice rising. "I thought so! I mean, we did some research, and the lady at the historical society told us you lived here. That your name was Serena."

Serena held the thin paper toward Lucy. "And since the letter was at your house, maybe the diary is at mine!" She withdrew her hand. "Um, could I show this to my mom?"

Lucy held her breath. *What if they take the letter and never give it back? What if Serena's mom doesn't want a stranger snooping though her house looking for personal belongings?*

"I could ask my mom if we could search for the diary tomorrow. Together. I mean, if you'd want to share this with me, too," Serena continued.

"Oh yes," Lucy answered. She didn't bring the key out of her shoulder bag, and Serena didn't mention it. "I think it would be cool for two girls to find it together. I mean, two girls wrote it together, after all."

"I'll be careful with the letter," Serena promised.

Lucy looked deep into her eyes and hoped she could trust her. "One last thing," she said. "If you don't mind. I think it's fine to tell your mom, but, well, please don't mention it to anyone else. Mary and the first Serena wanted it to be a secret, you know, and I'd like to honor that."

"No problem," Serena said. "It's past my curfew. I'll call you in the morning and let you know what my mom says."

"Okay! Talk with you then." Lucy's eyes creased with

happiness, the smile spreading all over her face as she started home.

"Hey, Lucy!" Serena called after her. "What's your phone number?"

Lucy stopped. What *was* her phone number? She'd never called it.

"I'll go home and lean out my window and yell it to you, okay?"

Serena waved her agreement. "Okay! I'll go into my room and wait. Bye!"

Lucy raced home and into the kitchen.

"How'd it go?" her dad asked.

"I'll tell ya in a minute," she answered. "Quick! What's our phone number?"

"It's 3578," her dad answered.

Lucy stopped. "Only four numbers?"

"Everyone on the Island has the same first three numbers, so they just use the last four."

Lucy nodded and ran up to her room, then opened her window. Sure enough, Serena waved out her back window. A thrill ran through Lucy's arms. Was this how Mary and the old Serena used to talk with each other? She called out, "The number is 3578."

Serena shouted, "Call you in the morning." At the sound of their voices, a nearby window slammed shut.

Lucy didn't care. It was happening! She was going to hold that diary in her own hands and read each and every word. She ran downstairs to give her dad and mom the fantastic report. Then she was off to bed to dream of the next day's adventure.

🌂 🌂 🌂

"So anyway, my mom said you can come over this morning if you want to look for the diary." Serena had phoned at ten o'clock on the dot.

"Do I want to? Of course! Yes!" Lucy said. "I'll ask my mom."

Her mom was wiping dishes in the kitchen. After talking with Serena's mom for a minute, she agreed that Lucy could go over.

Lucy ran upstairs, tucked the key into her shorts pocket, grabbed the two-way radio, and chugged out the door.

Serena was waiting for her at the front door.

"Come on up to my room." After introducing Lucy to her mother, Serena grabbed Lucy's sweaty hand just like an old friend would and ran upstairs. Serena's room was at the top of the house, in the converted attic.

A fuzzy, gray-eyed kitten meowed hello as Lucy walked in. Lucy tickled the kitty under her chin as she scanned over the room. A couple of posters of bands Lucy'd never heard of covered Serena's walls, and Lucy spied a mood ring on the dresser. Lucy held back a smile and twisted her own ring on her left hand, which was red for excitement. Cool. They were a lot alike!

She noticed a blue book sitting on the table beside Serena's bed. It said *Holy Bible*.

A filmy white curtain billowed like a small sail in front of the window, the window Serena had called out of last night. Lucy got a good feeling in her room. It was cozy.

"Sorry it's a mess," Serena said, opening one of two cubby doors on either side of her room. She kicked dirty clothes into the cubby, which was only a few feet tall because of the slope of the roof. Serena slammed the cubby door, trapping the clothes behind it.

From her top dresser drawer she pulled the letter out. "Where should we look first?" She handed the letter to Lucy, who held back for a minute before taking it. *Who does it really belong to?*

"Which room was your great-grandmother's?" Lucy asked. "It would be a good place to start."

"I don't know," Serena said. "I asked my mom, and she said she didn't know her grandmother hardly at all. She died before my mom was born. She didn't know where to look."

"Well, I found the diary key in a dresser that was built into the wall. In a false back. Do you have any built-in dressers?" Lucy asked. The two-way radio tugged at her shorts; she unclipped it and set it on Serena's bed.

"There's one in my brother's room."

"Would he let us look?" Lucy stood up. "It's a good place to start."

"He's not home." Serena thought for a minute. "He probably wouldn't mind, though. After all, it's a good cause." She put her finger to her lips. "Follow me."

The two of them tiptoed down the hall and into Serena's brother's room. In the far corner was a built-in dresser.

"You'd better look," Lucy said. Man, she didn't want to

be going through some stranger's stuff.

Serena pulled every drawer out and checked for false backs. None.

They tiptoed out. "What next?" Serena asked. She looked discouraged already.

"Don't lose hope!" Lucy took Serena's hand and tried to keep their spirits up. "We just started! Are there any other bedrooms?"

"Only my mom and dad's. And there aren't any built-in dressers in there. But there is a built-in china cabinet in the dining room."

Lucy snapped her fingers. "That must be it!"

The two girls raced downstairs and carefully removed every dish and crystal goblet from the cabinet. They searched each corner and knocked on the wood, listening carefully for a hollow sound. Nothing.

After setting all the dishes back in their places, the girls trudged upstairs again.

"I guess I'd better head home for lunch," Lucy said. "I told my mom I'd be back by noon."

"Do you think we're going to find it?" Serena asked as she walked Lucy to the door.

"If we can think of where else to look," Lucy said. *And if it's still here*, she thought, but she didn't say it. "Maybe we can look again after lunch."

"Okay," Serena agreed. "Here's my number." She wrote her number on the inside of Lucy's palm with a blue ballpoint pen. "Call me if you think of anything."

Lucy slogged down Marine Way and turned onto Pebble Road.

"Find anything?" Her mom met her at the door.

"Nah," Lucy said. She nibbled on a peanut-butter-and-jelly sandwich and fizzed down a Dr Pepper. As she ate, she unfolded the letter and read it again. She was really stuck.

Well, Mom and Dad pray. So does Claudette.

Lucy closed her eyes. "Dear God," she whispered. "Help me to figure this out. I mean, if you want me to, that is. Amen."

She stared at the letter, rereading each word. A mystery had to have clues. Where were the clues?

Was *gumdrop* a clue? A candy jar?

Nah.

It was at Serena's house, at least in 1932, for sure. The letter said so. She read it again. *High places.* It seemed kind of . . . well, weird.

The attic is a high place! Lucy's eyes scanned the page again. Serena's room?

Potatoes. Was that a clue?

Nobody kept potatoes in an attic.

Lucy read it again. *Walk all over our words.* That's a strange way to say something. It *must* be a clue! She gulped down the bite in her mouth and picked up the phone. She quickly hung it up again. *Dad's on the Internet—doing research on his lunch break, as usual.*

Lucy dumped her plate into the sink and saw her mom's two-way radio. A smile slowly spread across her face. She'd left *her* half in Serena's room!

"Serena!" she called over her mother's radio several times. "Serena!"

A minute later an answer crackled back. "Um, yes? Is

that you, Lucy? Am I working this right?"

"You definitely are," Lucy said. "And now we're like real detectives! I think I know where the diary could be. Can I come over in a few minutes?"

"Anytime," Serena's voice crackled over the radio. "In fact, the sooner the better!"

Grandma Peggy Trouble

Tuesday afternoon . . .

As soon as Lucy arrived, they ran straight into Serena's room and slammed the door.

"Look!" Lucy's long, thin fingers shook as she unfolded the letter and showed the clues in the letter to Serena.

"Hey!" Serena said. " 'Walk all over our words' could mean the diary's under the floor!"

"You got it," Lucy agreed.

Serena plunked down on her bed. "It's not like my mom and dad are going to let us rip up the entire floor in my bedroom to get to it."

"Oh." Lucy plunked down beside her.

The growing heat of the day smothered the hot attic.

Serena popped up. "You know, there are a few loose floorboards in the cubbies, where I shoved my dirty clothes.

They used them to stuff insulation down into the walls of the house. I don't know when they did that, but there's always a chance!"

Lucy could feel her excitement growing. "Yeah! 'Cause it's not likely your great-great-grandmother was going to let the diary girls rip up the floors, either."

"You're right!" Serena turned toward Lucy. "The cubbies are a mess. I mean, really. So don't be grossed out."

"Oh yeah, like I'm a Merry Maid," Lucy giggled. "Let's go!"

They stepped into the dimly lit cubby to the left and moved out Serena's beach chair and her big yellow beach umbrella.

"Oh, this is so cool." Lucy unfolded it.

"I get too dark if I stay in the sun too long," Serena said.

"I wish," Lucy said. "Come on, let's keep working."

Serena threw out two damp towels that smelled slightly moldy and one sandal with a broken strap. When they cleared the floor, she found the loose floorboard and peeled it back. Just pink fluffy insulation. And gray fluff. No diary.

Serena let the board fall back into place. *"Nada,"* she said.

They stuffed everything back into the cubby except the yellow umbrella, which Lucy had left leaning against Serena's bed. Racing, they cleared out the second cubby. Serena peeled back the loose set of floorboards.

More insulation. They sat down together.

"It's not here," Serena sighed.

"Come on, let's keep at it. We're detectives, remember?"

Lucy encouraged her new friend. "We'll work together. Till we find it. And I just feel like it's here," Lucy said. She cupped her chin in her hands.

"Okay," Serena said.

Lucy snapped her fingers. "Let's get some gloves!"

"Gloves?" Serena asked.

"Yeah. The insulation is prickly. If we get some gloves, we can look down underneath it."

Serena looked at her admiringly. "You have great ideas!" The two of them dashed downstairs into the bathroom and dug under the sink for Serena's mother's yellow rubber cleaning gloves. When they found them, Serena slipped her hands into them and they raced back upstairs. While she did, Lucy tied Serena's bandanna around her mouth and nose.

"You goof!" Serena said.

"I don't want to breathe insulation fibers," Lucy said, giggling.

Serena went to the first cubby and rummaged around. Nothing.

The girls stepped over to the second cubby, and Serena lifted one of the loose boards, then the next, feeling around in the cloudy piles of old insulation.

Lucy heard a thud as Serena's hand struck something.

She held her breath, fully expecting to see even more pink and gray fuzzy insulation.

Instead she saw the diary.

"It's here!" Serena screamed, jumping up and down. "It's here and we found it and nobody else did!" She blew it off and handed it to Lucy. "Here, you should open it. You found the letter."

"No, you should open it," Lucy insisted. "It was your great-grandma's." She unselfishly handed over the key, too.

They sat side by side with the yellow umbrella propped open over their heads, leaning on Serena's bed.

"Thank you for letting me go first," Serena said. "It's really nice." She inserted the key, twisted it, and cracked open the cover. A sweet, dusty smell, like the powder on a stick of gum, puffed into the air.

Lucy looked over her shoulder and read aloud: *"The Diary of Serena and Mary, Faithful Friends. Summertime, 1932."*

"Look!" Serena said. "There's a pouch in the back with stuff in it!"

The girls screamed again and shortly were interrupted by a sharp rap on the door. Serena closed the diary and slid it under her pillow.

"Girls?" Serena's mother entered the room.

"Hi, Mom. I thought you were Roberto. Guess what— we found it!" Serena pulled the diary out from under her pillowcase.

Her mother took the diary in her hands and slowly traced her fingers over the loose binding.

Be careful, Lucy thought, *or it might fall apart!* Of course she didn't say it.

"I thought you might have found it," her mom smiled. "I wanted to talk with you about that." She sat down on the desk chair next to them. Serena reached over and retracted the umbrella from over their heads.

This does not *sound good.* Sweat drops trickled down Lucy's back in unstoppable rhythms. Suddenly *no* breeze blew in through Serena's triangle-shaped windows.

"Well, I was thinking about it, and I thought we should ask Grandma Peggy if it's all right if you two read this diary, or if she wants to keep it for herself."

"What?" Serena asked.

Lucy said nothing, but her stomach started to ache.

"I know, I know," Serena's mother said. "I just got to thinking, it was her mom and all, and her mom died young, and I know how I would feel."

"I guess I see that," Serena said.

Lucy hated to admit it, but she could see it, too. After all, if it were something that had belonged to *her* Grammy's mother, she'd probably want to do what was right by Grammy, too.

Lucy's voice squeaked out like a poorly tuned flute. "Do you think she'll want to keep it?"

"I don't know. Serena and I are going over town tonight to go shopping, and I'll talk with her in person while we're on the mainland."

Lucy held out the letter and the key. "Here are these, too." Her words crumbled like dry bread in her mouth.

"Thank you. You're a good girl." Serena's mother shut the door behind her.

"What do you think she'll do?" Lucy asked.

"I don't know," Serena answered. "She's a nice grandma, though, and lots of fun. She also loved her mother."

Serena stood up and pulled Lucy from the bed. "Come

on, there's nothing we can do about it now, and speaking of fun, let's go have some!"

Lucy's eyebrows rose. "What kind of fun?"

"Now it's my turn for a good idea. Ever been in a pedal boat?" Serena asked.

"No," Lucy said with a smile. "But I like boats."

"Let's go!"

🍄 🍄 🍄

A couple of minutes later they arrived at the dock. Lucy scanned the tied-up boats. *Cool!*

"We want a pedal boat for an hour," Serena told the man behind the counter of Jack's Shack on the Green Pleasure Pier. The greasy, doughy smell of fish and chips snaked its way down the pier and tickled Lucy's nose.

"Well, look who's here."

Lucy turned around. It was Crabby Girl.

"Hi, Julie!"

A second girl stood next to Crabby, whose real name was apparently Julie.

"Pedal boats?" Julie asked. She directed her question toward Serena but stared at Lucy.

"Yeah, Lucy's never been on them. Have you met Lucy?" Serena introduced them all around.

"Well, since she's new, maybe she'll want to make even more friends." Julie's words sounded nice, but her eyes burned hot. "She can go in a pedal boat with Betsy, and I'll go with you."

"All right," Serena said.

What? Lucy couldn't believe Serena had agreed to that. Before she knew it, she sat next to Betsy in a yellow boat, pedaling with both feet.

"Where are you from?" Betsy asked, tucking her long braids into the back of her T-shirt.

"Washington State," Lucy said. She noticed Julie had steered herself and Serena to the other side of the harbor.

"I'm from L.A.," Betsy said, "but I live here all summer." She pedaled backward. "Want to throw popcorn in the water?" She held out a small plastic bag of stale popcorn.

Lucy glanced up. Wasn't that littering? Why would you do it, anyway? "Sure," she said, shaking her head.

"Watch," Betsy said. She tossed a few kernels into the water, and two huge fish flew to the surface and gulped them down.

"Whoa!" Lucy laughed. "Can I try?" She tossed a few kernels in, and a few fishy schoolmates joined the first two.

"I was new last year. I'm still kind of new," Betsy said.

"And you're Julie's friend?" Lucy asked with disbelief.

"When she wants to be," Betsy said with a smile.

Lucy smiled back. After another half hour of sun and pedaling, they met Julie and Serena at the dock.

"We're off to the beach. Wanna come?" Julie asked Serena. She didn't look at Lucy.

"No, we've got other plans," Serena answered.

We do? Lucy wondered. But before Julie could invite herself along, Lucy said, "Good-bye, Betsy. Great to meet you." She looked at Julie. "Good-bye!"

Lucy and Serena strolled down the Pleasure Pier.

Should I say anything about her ditching me for Julie?
Lucy wondered.

"Isn't Betsy great?" Serena put her arm through Lucy's
to guide her left. "What a cool thing for you to get to meet
someone else!"

"Yeah," Lucy said. Betsy had been great, after all. And
maybe Serena hadn't meant to abandon her. "Where are we
going?"

"Sweet Dreams," Serena said. "My treat."

"Ah, excuse me . . ." Lucy said. She tried to tell Serena
she didn't like ice cream—it hurt her teeth—but Serena
pulled her into the pink-and-yellow-striped shop.

"Hi, Jake," Serena called out.

Lucy gazed at Jake, and Jake gazed back.

"Hi, Serena," he said. His eyes never left Lucy.

"I'll take a peppermint cone. What do you want?" she
asked Lucy.

"I . . . um, I don't like ice cream," Lucy said.

"I'll bet you'll like this ice cream," Jake challenged. "Try
it."

"I don't like any ice cream." Lucy wasn't going to give
in. Even if he had dark brown eyes and a nice smile that
crinkled into his tanned face. He looked like her cousin
Ned, who was thirteen. "Not even chocolate-covered
cherry?" he asked. "It's my favorite."

She shook her head. "Is it okay if I order something
else?" she asked Serena.

Serena nodded.

"Dr Pepper, please," Lucy insisted sweetly.

"Later, girls," Jake said after they had paid. "Hope to

see you around," he called out, smiling at Lucy again.

On the way back to Lucy's house, Serena slurped the last melted ice cream from her cone and said, "Jake's family owns that shop." She crunched the last of the cone. "I think Jake liked you."

"Hah!" Lucy elbowed Serena playfully as they arrived at Lucy's house. Serena elbowed her back with a laugh.

"I'm going over town tonight, and I'll be back tomorrow night," Serena said. "I'll call you when I get home and let you know what Grandma Peggy said."

The sick ache crawled back into Lucy's stomach. Maybe it was the Dr Pepper. Or maybe it was because the day had started with such promise and now she had no letter, no key, and no diary.

"Call me right away," Lucy said. "The second you walk in the door."

"I promise," Serena said. "Cross my heart."

Urgent Messages

Wednesday afternoon . . .

Since Serena was going to be gone, Lucy decided to spend the next day with her parents on the *Gale Forces*, the small boat the university kept for personal use. It might be fun. She checked the calendar on the fridge on the way out of the house. Two days till she had to call Grammy and let her know if she was coming back for the summer.

The three of them suited up before motoring an hour out into the channel for her dad to take deep-water kelp samples. Lucy loved to squeeze the knobby bulbs on the golden kelp stalks but tossed them aside after a while.

She rubbed sunscreen over her arms and hoped for the best. When she got home she wanted to have some color. She stared out over the open water, the blue surface choppy with whitecaps.

Her mom and dad were so silent. It was weird. Like the old times, when they were fighting.

"I think I'll go below and get something to drink," she

Urgent Messages

Wednesday afternoon . . .

Since Serena was going to be gone, Lucy decided to spend the next day with her parents on the *Gale Forces*, the small boat the university kept for personal use. It might be fun. She checked the calendar on the fridge on the way out of the house. Two days till she had to call Grammy and let her know if she was coming back for the summer.

The three of them suited up before motoring an hour out into the channel for her dad to take deep-water kelp samples. Lucy loved to squeeze the knobby bulbs on the golden kelp stalks but tossed them aside after a while.

She rubbed sunscreen over her arms and hoped for the best. When she got home she wanted to have some color. She stared out over the open water, the blue surface choppy with whitecaps.

Her mom and dad were so silent. It was weird. Like the old times, when they were fighting.

"I think I'll go below and get something to drink," she

said. "Anyone want anything?"

"No thanks," they both answered at once, neither looking at each other or at her.

Mama mia. The fighting was back. No sense hanging around to watch.

Lucy went below deck and chugged some water, then tore off a piece of beef jerky. It was tough and tasteless. She spit it into the garbage pail nailed to the floor. Then she stepped up the stairs and could hear heated voices between her parents. Her mom's arm waved and her dad's voice, though low, still growled.

All at once, they must have sensed she was there. They stopped in midsentence and looked at her.

"I guess I'll go back down to read," she said. She didn't wait for an answer, but turned back and stomped downstairs.

So much for a tan. And so much for a "new life."

Lucy buried herself in her book. When she finished it, she ventured up to the deck again.

This time her parents were sitting near one another, laughing.

"Want to fish?" Dad asked.

"I suppose," Lucy said. "I'd like to catch a swordfish." *Before I go home for the summer,* she thought.

Her dad helped her cast while her mother brought out a couple of ham sandwiches on soft potato rolls.

The day grew brighter as the late-afternoon sun gleamed off of the shiny paint of their boat.

Lucy had to say something. She wiped her forehead with a beach towel. "So, are you over your fight?"

Her parents glanced at each other.

"Yes," her mother said. "It was a disagreement, not a fight, Lucy."

"I couldn't tell the difference." Lucy's heart hurt like it did in the old days when she'd covered her head with a pillow so she couldn't hear their angry voices.

"Daddy and I are still learning to work together, and just because we disagree does not mean we're going to separate again or get a divorce."

"Well, I wish someone would have told me you weren't angry anymore. It's hard to go on all peachy like nothing happened." Lucy set down her fishing rod.

"Like you wanted Mom to do after yelling at her the other day because you had to baby-sit Claudette?" Dad said.

Even though her mom looked down, Lucy saw the sadness in her eyes.

Like a fishhook in her hand, those words stung. *I guess that's right. I did the same thing. I was angry, and when it all blew over I never said I was sorry.*

She went over to her mother, hugging her with both arms for the first time in a long time. "I'm sorry, Mom."

"I know you are," her mom said, hugging Lucy back. She didn't let go right away, like she usually did.

Maybe it will be a new life, like they promised. At least the hope of one was near enough to feel it. She'd give it a chance.

Over her shoulder, Lucy spied the *Catalina Express* zipping across the channel, coming from the mainland back to the Island. She pulled back. "Hey! Maybe Serena and her mother are on that one!"

Her dad checked his watch. "They'll beat us back, if they are. I've got a couple of more things to do, and then we'll head in."

An hour and a half later they opened the door, and Lucy ran straight for the phone. "You have two messages," the voice mail operator announced.

She pressed the number 1 on the key pad, then listened for the first message. It was Serena.

"Hi, Lucy, it's Serena. Guess what? I talked with my grandma. We're putting our stuff away and then eating dinner. I think I'd better tell you this in person, so come on over about seven. Bye!"

Oh man, what had her grandma said? Lucy checked her watch. Only five o'clock now—two more hours.

Lucy deleted the message, then pushed number 1 on the key pad again. Second message.

"Hi, Lucy. It's Katie—you know, your cousin in need and a friend indeed?"

Katie! Lucy's heart double-timed as she gripped the phone with both hands. She hadn't talked to her since she'd left home.

Katie giggled before continuing. "My mom is doing better, although they're working me to death, as you can imagine. Come home and rescue me! I'm calling to say I have tons of fun planned for us, especially for your birthday next week. It will be great. I'm waiting to hear for sure that you're coming back. Grammy said you probably would come. Don't wait too long, because I have to firm up our plans! Call me soon. Bye!"

Lucy deleted the message before hanging up the phone. Worry gripped her stomach. What *was* she going to do? She could hear her mom and dad bustling in the background, her mom humming.

"Come help me with dinner, you two lazy bums," Dad called out in a happy voice.

She decided not to tell her parents about the last message. Not yet, anyway.

Meet Me at the Beach

Wednesday evening . . .

An hour and a half later, Lucy set her fork down on her plate and pushed the plate aside. "I'll do the dishes," she offered. "That way you guys can play chess if you want to."

Her mother set the dirty pan down on the counter top. "That's nice, Lucy," she said. "Are you feeling well? Do you want us to buy something for you?" she teased.

"Ah, come on, I clean up once in a while. I've got twenty minutes before I can go to Serena's, anyway."

"Nervous?" her dad asked before leaving the room.

"Yeah," Lucy admitted. Not only did she have the diary issue, but she'd have to call Katie back soon, too.

"This summer promises to be lovely, all of us together," her mom said. Lucy turned toward the sink so she didn't have to look her mother in the eye. No one had mentioned a word about Lucy leaving or staying—except Katie, of course—since their luncheon on Sunday.

Lucy stood next to the sink, soaping dishes and stacking them in the old wire dish drainer. The backs of her legs were bright pink with sun, where she forgot to put on sunscreen. The skin was tight and hurt when she walked. Lucy'd have to leave early and walk more slowly. As she wrung out the dishrag, she watched the town through the kitchen window. Boaters and fishermen tied up for the night, and skiffs bobbed merrily from wave to wave.

"I'm leaving now." She kissed her dad's cheek on her way out. Tiny beard hairs tickled her lower lip.

"Take the radio. Be home by eight."

The backs of her legs were really hurting now. The lotion she'd put on before dinner hadn't helped much.

As soon as she knocked on the door, Serena opened it up and smiled widely. *Good!*

"Come on upstairs," Serena said. "My mom is on the phone, but she said she'll come up as soon as she's done talking."

Once they got there, Lucy sat stiffly on Serena's bed.

"Are you upset or something? I mean, you're sitting kind of weird," Serena explained.

"Oh, that," Lucy said. "I got sunburned today."

"Oh, let me get you some aloe vera spray." Serena left her room, and Lucy heard her rummaging around in the bathroom cupboards near the foot of the stairs. Serena's room looked pretty much like it had yesterday, except there were shopping bags in the corner. Serena's kitty jumped up on the bed and onto Lucy's lap. Lucy petted her, grief over her dog Jupiter's recent death beating her heart again till she shook her head clear, reminding herself to not think about it.

"Here." Serena shooed the cat away. "I'll spray this on you."

Lucy stood up while Serena spritzed some aloe vera on her legs.

Aaahh. It did feel good. Really good.

"Thank you," Lucy said with sincerity. "Where can I buy some of this?"

"You can keep the bottle," Serena said.

"No, it's okay," Lucy said.

"Really," Serena said. "We have others." She put the bottle into Lucy's hands. "You know, we're going to be sharing a lot together anyway. The letter. The key. The diary."

"The diary!" Lucy said. "You mean your grandma said we could keep it?"

"Yes!" Serena said. "I could hardly wait to tell you. Grandma Peggy didn't even read it first, even though my mom told her she could if she wanted. She said her mother and Mary meant for the people who solved the mystery to get the prize, and she knew I'd take really, really good care of it and do like the letter said. It made her happy that her mom's diary was something I could share." Serena looked at Lucy. "With you, of course."

"Where is it?" Lucy asked. She glanced around Serena's room. No sign of the diary.

"My mom still has it. She'll bring it up in a minute."

Serena sat on the floor, where Lucy now sat, too, more comfortably.

Serena stuffed a softball T-shirt from her floor under her bed. "I hated softball. I stunk."

"Oh. I kind of like sports."

"You're probably good at them." Serena twisted her thick, long hair into a bun and secured it with chopsticks from the floor.

Lucy tucked her curls behind her ears. She'd never been able to twist her hair before. Stray curls always jutted out, making her look like she'd just survived a windstorm.

"I'd like to try kickboxing," Lucy said, her mind still on sports.

"Kickboxing!" Serena said. "You walked up to my house without knowing me, and now you want to try kickboxing. You're so brave! Aren't you afraid of anything?"

Lucy stared at her hands and twisted her rings. "Yes, I am," Lucy said. She didn't mention what she was afraid of, though. "You have beautiful hair," she said instead.

Serena smiled. "Part of my Mexican heritage," she said. Lucy smiled back, warmth flowing between them.

"Hey, girls." Serena's mother knocked on the door. When she opened it to come in, Lucy could hear Spanish-language TV downstairs. Mrs. Romero closed the door behind her and sat on a chair near the girls.

Lucy's heart jumped when she saw the red leather diary in her hand.

"I guess Serena told you that Grandma Peggy said you could keep the diary. And I have a great idea."

Lucy glanced at Serena, who shrugged her shoulders as

if to say, "I have no idea what she's talking about."

"Well, the diary was written slowly, week by week over the summer," Serena's mom said. "And it struck me that it would be kind of nice, and respectful of *my* grandma, if you two girls read it week by week over the summer, too. Not racing through it like gulping down a fast-food meal, but taking your time and savoring it instead."

Lucy kept her eyes steady and waited for Serena to answer.

Serena took a deep breath. "Well, Mom, they didn't actually *say* anything about that in the letter."

Mrs. Romero didn't answer. She still held the diary and made no move to hand it over.

"How about if we find somewhere special to read it instead?" Serena said. "Just the two of us, and we keep it private and a secret like the diary girls told us to? Would that work? It would be respectful even if we didn't read it slowly," Serena finished.

Lucy nodded. *Great idea!*

"All right," Mrs. Romero agreed. She handed the diary to Lucy and turned to leave. "Have fun, girls!" She giggled, and the girls giggled with her.

Lucy ran her fingers over the cover and thought about her time with her mom earlier in the day. "When should we read it? Where? How can we find a special place like we told your mom?" she asked. Her watch alarm beeped. Ten minutes till eight.

"I don't know," Serena said. "I . . . I didn't know what else to say, but I didn't really have anywhere in mind, either. Let's think of someplace fast!"

"I have to go home now," Lucy wailed, spending all of her willpower to not open the diary.

"If we both think hard, we'll think of it by tomorrow afternoon."

"Afternoon?" Lucy said.

Serena said, "I already promised to meet the girls at the beach on Thursday morning. Before we found the diary. A few more hours won't matter. After all, at least now we found the diary, and we know we get to keep it."

"That's true," Lucy admitted. "Let's promise we'll only read it together and not show anyone else the inside. Like the letter said. Is that okay with you?"

"Yes," Serena said. "I promise." She drew an X over her heart.

"I promise, too," Lucy said.

"Would it be okay if I showed it to my mom before we read it, too?" Lucy asked. "I promise we won't open it. I'll only show her the outside. Your mom has had a chance to hold it, and my mom helped me find your address and everything. I could keep it, just for tonight, and if you want you can keep the key so you know I won't read it."

"No, you don't have to give me the key!" Serena said. "Of course your mom should see it! You were nice enough to let my mom keep it for a whole day and night! Let's keep the diary, the key, and the letter together from now on. We can take turns. You take it home tonight, and take this home, too." She put the pink bottle of aloe vera in a little fishnet bag and handed it to Lucy.

Wow, even her bags are stylish. Lucy grinned. She put the diary, the letter, and the key in with the bottle, and the two of them headed downstairs.

"Hey! Why don't you meet us at the beach in the morning?"

"I already promised to baby-sit Claudette," Lucy said. "Before we found the diary."

"Why don't you bring her? Betsy's little sister comes, too."

Lucy wavered. "Are you sure?" *Crabby will probably be there.*

"Come on, it will be fun to have you there."

"Okay," Lucy agreed.

"The other girls will be glad to see you, too, I'm sure," Serena said.

Lucy's mouth felt like sticky rice. "The other girls don't know about the diary, though, right?"

"Right," Serena answered. "And it will stay our secret."

Make a Choice

Thursday morning . . . .

"Thank you." Lucy's mother gently squeezed Lucy's shoulder as she stepped into the pea-sized laundry room.

"For what?" Lucy ran her hands over the crisp sheet as she folded it, erasing a large wrinkle.

"For doing the laundry. And for not having a fit when Dad told you we have to go into the interior today to do research."

"Oh. That." The words felt flat in her mouth. Baby-sitting Claudette in the morning and a research trip in the afternoon and evening. The interior of the Island was empty, rocky, jagged land. There was a pretty lake in one place, and a horse stable farther along, but they weren't going to any of the fun places today. Just the dried-out crust of the land, hot and empty.

"I know how much you've been looking forward to getting together with Serena again," her mother said. "I'm glad you have a friend. At least you'll get to be with her at the beach today."

Along with everyone else, Lucy thought. But after all, she hadn't had to do too much for her mom and dad since she was here.

"I've been praying you'd find a good friend here," her mother said.

Praying.

Lucy handed a stack of clean linens to her mother. They smelled like sunshine and jasmine after hanging on the backyard clothesline. "I prayed once, too," she said.

"You did?"

"Yes," Lucy said. "I prayed that we'd find the diary."

"And you did."

Lucy nodded. "We did."

Her dad knocked on the door. "I'm leaving. Brent Kingsley is here, and he's dropped Claudette off. I'll be back at one o'clock to pick all of you up."

"Thanks." Her mother smooched her dad. Lucy grinned.

"I'd better get upstairs before Claudette eats all of my Jelly Bellies," she said. "We'll be back after lunch—" she sighed—"ready to go inland with you and Daddy."

Her mom handed Lucy a folded twenty-dollar bill. "Buy something for Serena, too. It's my treat. Take your radio."

Lucy balanced a stack of clean clothes on her head, trudging up the stairs like an African queen. As soon as she opened the door to her room, she gasped. Claudette held the diary!

"Claudette! You didn't open that, did you?"

Claudette let go of the diary, which clattered to the floor. "No. No."

Lucy exhaled with relief. "Good. It's just that it's private between me and Serena. We promised each other we wouldn't let anyone else read it or see what was in it."

"Oh. I didn't know you guys were that special of friends." Claudette looked hurt and jealous. She looked at the diary Grammy had sent for Lucy to record all of her summer adventures, which still sat unopened on Lucy's night table.

"Can I see that one?"

Lucy sat down on the bed next to her. "Listen, I'll go with you to buy your own diary, okay? Then you can write whatever you want in it and show it to whoever you want, too."

"Really?" Claudette jumped up. "When?"

"Oh, maybe . . . tomorrow." Lucy checked her watch. "Come on, we'd better get to the beach."

"I can't swim, remember," Claudette reminded her.

"It's okay. There's supposed to be another girl your age there, so maybe you'll make a new friend." Lucy opened her ring drawer and slipped on her turquoise ring and mood ring. "Let's go!"

A few minutes later they approached Crescent Beach, and Lucy's tummy tickled. The other girls were packed together on the sand like drying fish. There wasn't much extra room around them. She hated always having to squeeze her way into the crowd.

"Hey, it's Lucy!"

Betsy waved at Lucy and Claudette. Right next to Betsy

sat a younger girl with braids like Betsy's.

"Hi." The girl waved to Claudette, who immediately sat down.

"Sit with me," Serena called to Lucy. She had her big yellow umbrella open and scooted so there was enough room for Lucy, too. "That way you won't get burned again."

Lucy smoothed her towel down. Then she looked up and saw Julie staring at her. Julie's eyes didn't look brown today; they looked black.

The eight girls chatted together for a couple of hours, dipping their feet and watching as the boats pulled in. Lucy waited for someone to talk with her, but no one said much. A cruise ship from Mexico left its passengers for the day, spilling tourists into the town. Lucy scooped sand into little piles with a shell and noticed almost everyone waited for Julie to talk. When she did, no matter what the topic of conversation, from boys to books, they answered her with happy voices of agreement.

Then things got definitely worse.

"Did you know Serena and Lucy have a private old diary they can't show to anyone else?" Claudette announced.

Aaahh! Was there *any* way Lucy could crawl inside one of the seashells and wash out to sea?

"Oh really?" Julie piped up. "I haven't heard anything about it. Tell us, Serena," she said sweetly, but her black eyes weren't sweet.

"It's nothing, an old thing my great-grandma left behind and Lucy found the key," Serena said. "You know what?" she changed the subject. "I'm getting kind of hungry. We've been here for, like, hours. I think I'll get lunch."

"Wait, I want to hear about the diary," Julie insisted. No one else said anything. Lucy was going to speak, but Julie leaped in again.

"I mean, we've been friends for years, Serena. We're Islanders." She glanced at Lucy. "Others aren't. It seems like you should share with us." Two of the girls moved closer to Julie.

Lucy watched Serena.

"My great-grandma said in the letter she wanted the diary to be private to the finder."

"She's dead, right? I mean, how would she ever know?" Julie pushed on. "I think you should share it with us if you want to be friends still. I mean, real friends share everything, right? And we'll be here forever," she looked at Lucy again. "Unlike *some* people."

"I'm hungry, too," Lucy said. "Let's go." She stood up and brushed sand crumbs off of her legs.

"We'd better get going, too," Betsy said to her sister. She slipped on her sandals and tugged the girl away from Claudette, who was blissfully unaware of the trouble she'd started.

Lucy smiled at Betsy, but she noticed that Betsy avoided her gaze.

"See you later, Betsy," Julie called out. "Maybe this afternoon we can all go boating. I mean, most of us." Julie turned toward Serena. "You'll have to make a choice who you want to be friends with. Because remember—friends

CROSS MY HEART

share. I don't want to hang out with people who don't share. Make a choice."

Serena smiled weakly and said good-bye, and then she, Claudette, and Lucy walked toward town.

"My mom gave us money for lunch," Lucy offered. "Can I buy something for you, too?"

"No thanks," Serena said. "Besides, I feel bad that I didn't ask you to stay for lunch the other day." She walked more slowly than usual, and her shoulders slumped.

"Don't worry about it!" Lucy said softly, taking her hand. "Come on, let me buy you some lunch. I want to!"

Serena nodded. They grabbed an outdoor table at Coney Island. Serena and Claudette ordered cheeseburgers; Lucy ordered clam strips.

"I didn't tell Claudette about the diary," Lucy said. "She saw it in my room."

"What's wrong with that?" Claudette asked.

"Nothing," Lucy and Serena answered at the same time.

"It's not your fault," Serena said after she sipped her drink.

"And I can't meet this afternoon, either," Lucy added. "I have to go to the interior with my dad."

Serena sighed. "Maybe it's just as well, anyway. I haven't thought of anywhere cool to open the diary. And I might need time to think."

Think about what? Sharing the diary? Lucy opened her mouth to speak, then noticed Serena push her cheeseburger away.

I don't want to add to her sadness right now.

82

"I'll think hard of somewhere great for us to read the diary," Lucy said. "I'll focus on it all afternoon so that we have someplace cool to make it even more special. You think about it, too."

"All right." Serena stood up. "I'd better get home. I'll call you tomorrow."

Lucy watched her walk away, then looked toward the bay. Kids were climbing into pedal boats. Lucy thought for sure Serena had already chosen to keep the diary just between the two of them. A tiny corner of her mind, however, wondered if Serena would be boating with the other girls that afternoon.

Chocolate-Covered Cherries

Friday morning . . . .

The next morning Lucy walked out into the backyard in her jammies, hoping to catch her mother in a good mood.

"You know how I spent the whole day with Claudette yesterday, right?"

"Right," her mom said, watering the jasmine bushes before the day's heat softened their blossoms.

"Well, I told her I'd buy a diary with her today. Do you think it would be okay if I asked her if we did it tomorrow?" A playful breeze ruffled through Lucy's hair. She looked up toward Serena's house but didn't hear or see anything special.

Her mother set the tin watering can down. "You want to see Serena right away, I suppose?"

"I want to make sure everything is okay. And see if she's thought of anywhere good to read the diary."

"Did you think of anywhere?"

Lucy stuck a tender blade of grass between her teeth, sucking out the juicy part from the root. "All I could think of was the beach. Since we're here on the Island, you know, and the beach is here. I wish I could think of someplace else to make it more special." She spit the grass out. "I hope we're still friends."

Mom began watering again. "I'm sure you are. I think you've gone above and beyond baby-sitting duties with Claudette this week, so it's okay with me if you wait. Do what you think is best." She glanced at Lucy. "Don't forget, we have to call Grammy tonight to let her know what you've decided about the summer. Would you like to talk about it first?"

Lucy looked straight at her mother. "We'll talk about it tonight. And then call."

Lucy went inside and dialed Claudette's mother. She told her she'd take Claudette another day, then walked upstairs to get dressed.

After pulling on jean-short overalls and a pink T-shirt, Lucy ran a comb through her hair. She stared over at Serena's house through the back window. She could see the white curtain billowing and wondered if Serena was thinking about her.

I should call her, but she promised she'd call me. Lucy's arms were heavy, and so was her heart. *And I promised I'd take Claudette today.*

Promises. Lucy lumbered back downstairs.

"Mrs. Kingsley?" she spoke into the phone receiver. "I've changed my mind. I'll come get Claudette in a few minutes."

✦ ✦ ✦

"Thanks for taking me," Claudette said. "I was really looking forward to it."

Lucy was glad that Mrs. Kingsley hadn't told Claudette that Lucy had almost changed her mind. "I'm glad to take you, kiddo," she said.

A half hour later the two of them strolled into Dove Books and Gifts.

"You girls okay?" Lucy's mother called over the two-way radio clipped to Lucy's belt.

"Yes, Mom," Lucy replied. She could hear her mother's paintbrushes clinking in the linseed oil jar. Working again. Lucy turned down the radio's volume.

"Do you think they'll have a diary here?" Claudette asked as they entered the store. "Hey, I have a new jump rope song. You want to hear it?"

"I don't think inside the store is a good idea. How about on the way home?" Lucy suggested. She scanned the street and the beach for anyone she knew. Even though the street was packed with tourists, she recognized no one. No Betsy. No Julie.

No Serena.

"Here's the one I want!" Claudette pointed to a diary. "It's pink and has purple hearts on it. And it has a key," she squealed. "Like yours!"

Lucy purchased the diary with her own money.

"My mom gave me some money to buy it," Claudette said.

Lucy ruffled Claudette's hair. "My treat."

Then they started home. Claudette reached up and took Lucy's hand in her own. Lucy let her hold it for a minute before pulling her own hand away.

"Let's go home up a new street for a change," Lucy said. "We might as well see a bit more of the town."

"We'll be here all summer to see the town, goosey," Claudette answered.

Will I? Lucy thought. At the top of the hill, she spied an old church, where someone was digging weeds in the front.

"Oh, what a pretty church," Claudette said. "Maybe we can go there on Sunday. Let's see what time it starts."

"All right," Lucy said. It didn't mean she was going to church. It just meant she was seeing what time it started. She stared at the cross on the church and felt a strangely familiar spark of warmth in her heart.

As she got closer, she could see that the bent-over person weeding the flower beds was a boy. Kind of close to her age, maybe a little older. She stepped by him to read the sign that told the service times.

As he looked up at her, her eyes opened wide. It was Jake—the boy who loved chocolate-covered-cherry ice cream!

"Hi, Dr Pepper," he said. His arms were tan and burnt at the same time. A pile of pulled weeds like a mini haystack withered next to him, and potted flowers patiently waited for a garden home.

"Um, hi," Lucy answered.

Jake pulled a glove off of his hand and wiped the sweat from his forehead.

I hope he doesn't want to shake hands with me, Lucy thought.

"If you tell me what your name is, I'll use it!" He smiled.

"Her name is Lucy, mine is Claudette. Guess what?" Claudette drew her diary out of the bag with a flourish. "I got a new diary! Lucy bought it for me. Isn't she nice?"

"Wow, that's a pretty diary," Jake said kindly. "Hi, Lucy. You *are* nice."

"Do you go to this church?" Claudette asked. "Because we want to know what time it starts."

"I do go to this church," Jake answered. "There are only a couple on the Island. Ours starts at ten o'clock."

"We've got to go now. Nice seeing you." Lucy tugged at Claudette's arm.

"Bye," Claudette said. She turned to Lucy. "Is he your boyfriend?"

Argh! She was sure Jake had heard Claudette. Lucy kept her head down. *Doom!*

"Claudette!" she whispered. "*Please* be quiet." When they got down the street, a bit more toward Claudette's house, Lucy said, "He is *not* my boyfriend. Please don't use that word in front of boys."

"Okay," Claudette said.

Lucy dropped Claudette off at home and rounded the

corner; it was a block or so to her own house. There was no message from Serena when she got home, so she plopped down in her room to read for a while as she waited for Serena to call. Surely she would call soon! Maybe she overslept. Maybe she had to help her mother.

Maybe she won't call, a voice inside Lucy's head said. She tried to ignore it.

A snack would be good. Lucy snapped open her Jelly Belly case and considered her choices. She decided to mix a chocolate jellybean and a cherry jellybean to see what chocolate-covered-cherry ice cream might taste like.

One Lonely Gull

An hour later, still no call.

"I guess I'll practice the piano," Lucy called out to her mother, who was in the next room painting. Mom grunted a reply, saying nothing else. Lucy sat down and thumbed through the music she'd brought, looking for something interesting. She'd only played once or twice all week.

She found the score to *Titanic* and played it for a while, getting almost all of the notes just right, although she'd played it only two or three times before. Her piano teacher at home, Miss Fear, had presented it to her as a joke when she'd found out Lucy would be spending a lot of time on boats this summer. Lucy wondered if Miss Fear had already filled her regular lesson time for the summer or if it was still open, in case she went home.

After running through the tune twice, Lucy's shoulders sagged; she exhaled loudly. *Face reality. Serena isn't going to call.*

Lucy got her mother's permission and logged on to her email. First she wrote Miss Fear a note, seeing how her summer was going and asking, casually, if her summer was busy with students.

Then she began a note to Katie.

Dear Katie, she tapped out. *Summer hasn't gone the way we planned, has it? Maybe we can still have a good time. I haven't said anything to my parents yet. . . .*

Lucy sensed a weighty, certain pressure on her heart. She stared at the blinking cursor on the computer screen, unable to continue. Glancing over at the counter top, she spied the pink aloe vera bottle Serena had given her. That wasn't something just anyone would have done.

Lucy clicked "Send Later" on her computer before logging off. She tried to call Serena, but the line was busy. She'd have to walk over instead.

She headed up Pebble Road and down Marine Way.

A loose root lay across the sidewalk, and she stumbled on it. A flash of anger overcame her; she grabbed the root and chucked it into a nearby bush. She reached the Romeros' door and knocked.

Serena's older brother, Roberto, answered the door. "Yes?"

"Is Serena here?" Lucy asked.

"No, I think she's at the beach with her friends."

Lucy's spirits dropped to the ground. Her eyes must have betrayed her emotion, because Roberto asked, "Are you okay?"

"I'm okay," Lucy said. "Thanks."

Roberto shut the door softly.

Lucy walked up the street one extra block. She wasn't ready to talk with her mom about this quite yet. She walked past the mission-style houses with green shutters, past the Spanish-style houses with brown-sugar stucco. She reached the top of the road and ended up at the church she and Claudette had stopped at earlier that morning.

The lawn looked cool and inviting, the flowers settled into their new home. Lucy sat down on the grass, on the gentle slope of a hill. She pulled a fresh stem from the ground, then chewed on the clean, rubbery root for a minute before closing her eyes.

The distance muffled the happy voices from the beach, the low rumble and spark of a few passing golf carts the only interruption to the quiet. The turf felt both soft and scratchy beneath Lucy's still-pink legs.

"God, remember me? If you're there, please answer. I know we haven't really, um, talked for a while. Even though I used to talk with you a lot. A long time ago. I do believe you heard me about finding the diary the other day. I do miss you. I hope we can be close again. Please show me what to do now. Thanks."

She sat another minute, then decided to head back to Pebble Road. It might be better to go an extra block around, taking the long way, in order to control the sadness she felt trying to escape from the deepest part in her chest.

She came around the corner toward Coney Island and saw the street-side tables covered with hungry lunchers.

Maybe I'll get a Dr Pepper. She felt inside her pocket to see if she had any cash.

As she located a dollar bill, she looked up, still about a

block away. There at a table sat Julie, Betsy, and some others . . . including Serena.

Lucy turned abruptly, losing herself in the noisy crowd before anyone could see her.

She jogged a block out of her way, making a wide loop around the others. She stopped for a minute, staring out at the choppy sea, wondering what to do next.

A group of sea gulls roosted on a clump of rocks just off shore, pecking at a dead fish. One gull with a bald patch of plucked feathers perched alone. Every time it tried to approach the others, one of the gulls chased it off. The stray bird ran away, flapping, alone again.

Lucy wanted to help the lonely bird but could think of nothing to do. She pulled her hat low over her eyes so no one could see the tears she couldn't hold back anymore.

Fine. If that was the way it was going to be with Serena, she'd go home and read the diary herself.

Open Your Eyes

Friday afternoon . . .

Lucy raced onto her porch, throwing herself into the swing. After tossing off her hat, she sat with her legs up, head tucked into her knees, and stared at the starry black space behind her tightly closed eyes. The swing rocked back and forth, its squeaking and squawking rhythmic and precise. Predictable. Unlike anything else in Lucy's life.

"Hi." Mom came out onto the porch. "Do you want lunch?"

"Uh-uh." Lucy's voice was muffled. She didn't look up.

Her mother stood silent for a minute before placing her hand on Lucy's sweaty curls. "Mind if I sit down with you for a minute?"

Lucy didn't say anything, but she scooted to the left. Her mother sat down on the swing, which groaned with the extra weight. It swung more slowly now, the squeaking sounding like cries.

Two choices battled inside Lucy's mind. One was to

open herself up to her mother, which she almost never did. The other was to be calm and sure, doing things the way she always did. Depending on herself. Taking control.

She wanted to lean into her mother. But she couldn't bring herself to do it. And she didn't understand why not.

She wiped the back of her hand across her cheek. "I saw Serena."

"Did you talk with her?" her mother asked.

Lucy shook her head. "No. She was eating lunch at Coney Island with Julie and Betsy and all of the others." *Good thing I didn't already decide to stay here.*

"What are you going to do next?"

"Go home," Lucy said. "Stay with Grammy for the summer." She watched as her mother's arms dropped to her side. Lucy turned away before she could know for sure if there were tears in her mom's eyes.

"Mom, I can't stay here all summer, baby-sitting Claudette and walking around the beach with the Island girls being so mean. Please understand. And I'm going to read the diary before I go. I think I deserve to. After all, I found the letter."

"Oh, Lucy," her mother said. "I know how bad you feel. But think about this before you read it."

Lucy spied her dad's golf cart coming down the road.

As she stood up, the swing screeched. "I did think about it," she said. "I'm going up to my room."

Snatching her hat from the corner of the porch, Lucy stepped into the house and up the stairs before her father could park the cart.

Once in her room, she shut the door and opened her

window, allowing her room to breathe out the stifling hot air and breathe in cool, fresh air from the outside. As she opened the screen, she stared at Serena's window, the white curtain billowing. *Why, Serena, why?* Fresh tears sprang to Lucy's eyes, and she threw herself on her bed.

Nothing ever works out for me. I try to do what's right for other people, and nobody is watching out for me.

She yanked her suitcase out from under her bed and unzipped it. She rummaged through the closet and took out some of her clothes, stacking them in the left-hand side of the suitcase. She opened the special jewelry drawer where she'd first found the letter and the key, then wrapped up her beaded necklace in a silken wrapper and set it into the suitcase. As she looked up at her bedside table, Lucy ran her finger over the top of the diary Grammy had sent to her. When her fingers touched the unwrapped Bible, her heart lurched with the same aching and longing she felt when she sang "Jesus Loves Me" on her floor the other day. Only stronger.

A few minutes later a soft knock came. "Can I come in?" Her dad's voice filtered through the door.

She slid the suitcase under her bed. "All right."

She sat on her bed. Her dad sat down beside her.

"I hear you had a disappointing experience today."

Lucy nodded, the tears flowing. The hard spot in her heart melted more easily with her dad.

"Serena was supposed to call me. She and I were going to read the diary," Lucy said. "But Julie was so mean to her and didn't want to be friends with her unless we shared the diary. Then today, no call. Instead, there she is with them. I guess she made her choice."

Dad nodded and stroked his beard. "I see. Is there any chance you might not know the whole story?"

"What whole story? Everyone I trust always abandons me in one way or another! I stick with them, they leave me." Lucy wanted to kick something . . . or crawl into her dad's lap. She didn't do either.

"She's not going to keep her end of the promise, so why should I keep mine? I should just read this thing."

Her dad was quiet, then said, "A promise isn't about the other person, Lucy. Keeping a promise you've made is about you."

"Dad, I don't know what you're talking about!"

"I've been thinking about promises lately. I'll be right back," he said. He stepped out of the room and reappeared a minute later.

"I found this before we left home. I'd been keeping it in my Bible," he said. A bent picture . . . an old picture. He handed it over to Lucy.

She drew in her breath when she saw it; it was the same ache she'd sensed when she'd touched her Bible, only more powerful. It was a picture of Mom, Dad, and Lucy at family camp all those years ago when they'd first become Christians.

In the picture a younger Lucy clutched a brand-new Tender Teddy that a teenaged camp counselor Lucy admired had given her. She'd seemed almost like a big sister. Lucy reached over and grabbed Tender Teddy again.

"Do you remember when we took that picture?" Dad

asked. He came across the room and sat next to her on the bed.

"Yes," Lucy said. "I remember."

"We'd all become Christians, met Jesus, and we were excited for a new life with Him."

"Yes," Lucy said. "But Jesus went away."

"Jesus never went away. What happened," her dad said, "was that your mother and I walked away from Him. We got so busy, so overwhelmed by life, that we didn't live as we should have. Not toward the Lord, not toward each other. Not toward you. I'm sorry."

"I didn't want to walk away," Lucy accused. "I practically begged to go to church. I practically begged," she said, tears fresh now, saying things she never said at the time. "I trusted you and Mom, and you guys left me out of the picture when you separated! I'm worried that everyone I ever love or ever like will abandon me!"

Her dad stroked her hair. "But they won't. Try to trust. Look at Mom and me—we're back together now, working things out, keeping the promise we made to each other when we got married. To stick together in better or worse. Is it important to you that we work to keep the promise?"

Lucy nodded. "Is that the promise you mean?"

"Yes, that and one other." He folded his hand over Lucy's. "All those years we walked away from Jesus, He never walked away from us. God promises He will never leave us or give us up. Once we're His, we're His forever. We walked away from Him, but He's been right there waiting for us to turn back to Him. He's been keeping His promise. If you open your eyes, you'll see Jesus waiting."

"I opened my eyes and saw Him before, when you two walked away. Claudette said if I trusted Jesus once, I'm still a Christian."

"That's true." Her dad stood up. "So the question is, are you willing to open your eyes and see Him now?"

Lucy stared at the camp picture again.

"No matter what you decide about the summer, Sparky," her dad said, "you can't run away from your troubles, can you?"

Lucy said nothing for a full minute. Then she nodded her agreement. "I have to talk to Serena, I guess. Even if she abandoned me."

"I love you," her dad said. "I know it's hard, but this summer might be a time to learn to trust the people you feel have let you down and see what happens."

"I love you, too, Daddy."

Her dad opened the door and stepped out, closing the door behind him.

No matter what kind of person anyone else is, I've decided to be a person who keeps her promises. I'm not going to read the diary.

Lucy set the red leather book, the old letter, and the key into Serena's fishnet bag before stepping in front of her dresser to straighten her hair.

As she stepped in front of the mirror, she closed her eyes. "God, who will take care of me if I do the right thing? Who will watch out for my best interests if I'm always doing the right thing for others? Who was there when my parents separated—and I'm still afraid they'll divorce. When the kids ignored me? When my dog Jupiter died?"

When she opened her eyes, they were drawn downward, but they still stared into the mirror. Halfway down Lucy's reflection, just across her chest, was the cross Claudette had stuck onto the mirror on Tuesday.

She traced the cross on her own chest; it landed right across her heart. Instead of marking an X across her heart as she normally did when she made a promise, she traced the cross. *A cross across my heart.* She traced the cross against her chest again. *Cross my heart.* God promised to never leave her. He'd stick by her no matter what.

"Cross my heart," she whispered. "For when I'm scared."

She picked up the bag and went to call Serena.

15

Saturdays

Late Friday afternoon . . .

Lucy went downstairs to dial Serena's number. Within one ring, Serena picked it up.

"Hello?"

"Hello, Serena? This is Lucy."

"I was just going to call you!" Serena answered. Lucy twisted the phone cord around her arm. Serena sounded like she meant it.

"You were? Well, I wanted to talk, and I wondered if we could talk in, ah, person."

"Sure! How about at the beach?"

Funny, I had thought the beach would be a good place to read the diary. A spear of pain poked Lucy's heart.

"Will anyone else be there?"

"I don't think so. We can go to Middle Beach. Hardly anyone ever hangs out there. Do you know where it is?"

"Yeah," Lucy said. "It's near where our boat is moored. Meet you there in ten minutes."

"Ten minutes! Can't wait!" Serena answered cheerily before clicking off the phone.

Lucy's tangled emotions worsened with each conversation. Good and bad, happy and sad, confused and knowing—they all twisted together in knots.

"I'm going to the beach," she told her parents on the way out the door.

"Not alone," her mother said.

"No, I'm going to meet Serena there," Lucy answered. "Okay?"

"Okay," her mom said. "I'll be praying for you."

Lucy felt her cheeks grow warm. "Thanks."

She puttered down the street, and the young boy next door waved at her. Lucy smiled, waving back. She popped in a few Jelly Bellies from a stash in her pocket before turning toward Middle Beach.

Stepping over the rocky fence separating the beach from the town, Lucy saw Serena already there, her big yellow beach umbrella stuck into the sand. Lucy went over and sat down next to her.

"Hi," she said. She set the fishnet bag down next to her. A sand crab crawled toward her, just like the one she'd seen on her first day at the beach when she first spied Serena and the others. Lucy took a deep breath. Might as well dive right in.

"I saw you at Coney Island," she said. "With the others. I thought you were going to call me."

"I was going to call you," Serena said. "I was getting ready to pick up the phone when you called me."

"I mean, I thought you were going to call me right away today."

"I'm sorry. I didn't mean I'd call you exactly first thing." Serena dug her toes into the sand. "I felt like I had to make things right with the others first before I could go on. I don't like it when people are mad."

"So are things right with them?" Lucy asked. She dug her toes into the sand, too, but a foot or two away from Serena's.

"Yes!" Serena brightened. "Isn't that great?"

Lucy's dream sank. "Great." She handed the diary, the letter, and the key over to Serena. "I guess you'll be wanting these."

Serena looked up. "What?"

"If you're going to share the diary with them."

Serena's mouth dropped open. "I didn't say I was going to share the diary with them! We talked it out, and Julie kind of understood how I felt about doing what my great-grandma had wanted. And about my promise to you. At least I'm not on the black list for now."

"She was so mean to you!" *And me.*

Serena blinked and thought before answering. "Julie's mom doesn't have much time for her since she got a new boyfriend."

"Oh. I'm sorry for her."

"Anyway, I wouldn't break my promise to you." Serena drew an X over her heart. "I keep my word." Serena looked at her. "Did you know I'm a Christian?"

"I thought maybe you were. I saw the Bible in your room."

"Are you a Christian?" Serena asked.

Lucy remembered Claudette saying that if Lucy had asked Jesus to be her Savior once, even if it was a long time ago, He was her Savior forever. "I am a Christian," she answered with a quiet smile. "But I'm just starting to figure out what that means."

"We can figure some things out together, you know, over the summer," Serena said. She moved closer to Lucy, under the umbrella.

"I'm not sure I'm going to be here all summer," Lucy said.

"Oh." Serena looked disappointed.

"It's just that, well, every summer my dad goes on these trips for research and I tag along. I never get to have a normal summer. With friends, parties, excitement . . . you know?"

Serena nodded. "You have me here."

"Well," Lucy said. *Might as well bring it all up.* "What about after we read the diary? I mean, you could go back to your old friends and I'm stuck."

"I wouldn't abandon you!" Serena sighed. "But talk about old friends. Talk about the same summer every year. Boooooring. I do the same things, with the same people, in exactly the same way every summer of my life. It's sickening. I'd give anything for one of your exciting summers."

"My exciting summers picking ferns or helping my dad hand-pollinate rare flowers? No thanks. That's boooooring. I'd give anything to be with friends all summer. That's exciting." Lucy stared at the diary, still in the bag. "You know, I have an idea. Maybe we could make this summer different. Exciting. For both of us."

Serena snapped to attention. "Really? How?"

"Remember what your mom said?"

"No," Serena frowned.

"She said we should read the diary slowly. You know, like the other Serena and Mary wrote it. It would be hard, though," Lucy said, "very hard not to read it all at once."

"Yeah, but we could do it. I know we could!" Serena said. "And my mom will be so glad we took her idea."

"We could make our own adventures. Every week!" Lucy said.

Serena leaped up. "Whatever they do . . ."

"We do," Lucy said.

"No matter how hard or embarrassing or crazy," Serena continued.

"Or risky!" Lucy finished. "We can do something the same, or almost the same, no matter what!"

"Great!" Serena agreed.

"And we'll stick together, promise?" Lucy said. "I would never make you choose between me and your other friends, like Julie said, because I don't think that's right. But I also don't want to be left alone," she said softly. "Do you understand?"

"I do understand. And I want us to keep the diary to ourselves, because that's what my great-grandma wanted. We'll stick together, even if we hang out with other girls, too, sometimes. Cross my heart," Serena said. Lucy smiled inside, thinking of her own cross across her heart. She'd share that with Serena someday.

Lucy wanted to show how much she appreciated Serena. "My Grammy sent me a summer diary. I'd be glad to share it with you. What if we write in it together? You know, a friendship diary. We can write all about our adventures this summer and put them in there. Totally honest, like Mary and Serena. Would you like to?"

"I'd love it! Another one of your great ideas, and it's so sweet of you to offer," Serena said. "Let's read one section of the old diary every week, like you said, till the end of the summer. And then write in ours!" She squeezed Lucy's hand. "It will be so fun!"

"How about we have to finish whatever our plan is by each Friday night, so we're ready for the next one on Saturday? We can call the day we have to be done with our adventure 'D Day,' for 'Diary Day.' Or 'Do it by this day or else!'"

"Great idea!" Serena said.

"When should we read the diary?" Lucy was ready to start reading now. "And where?"

Serena settled back down onto the sand. "Well, since you made the plan about reading it each week, could I decide when and where?"

Lucy nodded.

"We said we were going to open the diary in a special place. I kind of like the beach."

"Me too!" said Lucy.

"But is it special enough?"

"It could be," Lucy said. "I mean, maybe the girls wrote on this exact beach. It's possible."

"It's kind of cool being together under my yellow umbrella," Serena said. "After all, it's where we first opened the diary together in my room. It's where we're making our plan right now."

"True," Lucy agreed. "We read the diary and plan our next adventure under the umbrella, on the beach." She swallowed hard, looking at the diary. "When should we start reading?"

"Well, what day did you first find the letter?" Serena asked.

"Saturday," Lucy said. Her heart sank. Today was Friday. She really, really wanted to read it now.

"Well, how about if we read it on Saturdays then?" Serena suggested. "Every Saturday. Starting . . . tomorrow!"

"All right," Lucy agreed. It wouldn't be fair for her to get to pick everything. She didn't want to be bossy with her new friend.

Lucy glanced at the diary. "Do you think it would matter if we peeked at some of the stuff in the pocket in the front, you know, just to start, to get an idea?"

"I think getting a preview is all right," Serena said with a giggle. Serena twisted the key into the diary and opened the faded pink envelope glued to the front cover of the diary. She stuck her hand in and drew out some treasures. She handed half to Lucy.

"What do you have?" she asked. Lucy shuffled through her stack. "A party invitation, a cool one," she said. "A napkin with some writing on it. A piece of gold chain taped to a paper." She fingered the treasures, her heart bursting to figure out what these meant.

"I've got a folded-up, taped letter." Serena sniffed it. "It smells like perfume." She shuffled through some other things. "Hey! An airline ticket. Two of them! And a tiny wooden horse. Movie tickets."

They searched through the treasures for another minute and then carefully put them back. All except one folded piece of paper, which Lucy had held on to.

"Should I read it?" she asked.

Serena nodded.

Lucy unfolded the paper and read aloud. The words were written in two sections, like the letter that started all of this—first a set in scrolling writing and then one printed in blocks. There were only four lines.

"*Some days are cloudy, some have sun*
We'll walk together through every one
No matter what comes at summer's end
we'll always be two faithful friends.
FF
Mary and Serena"

Lucy folded the letter up and slid it into the envelope. Her hand lingered, wanting to turn the diary's first page, but also wanting to honor Serena's plan.

She closed the diary and gave it to Serena. "Your turn to keep it."

"Till tomorrow." Serena looked at the diary. "Faithful friends. I like that."

"Me too," Lucy said. She looked at Serena, shy for once. "We could be faithful friends, too, you know. Until summer's end, like the poem says."

"It's a deal," Serena said. "Faithful friends."

Serena folded up her umbrella before stepping onto the road toward their homes. "I'm going home to tell my mom that we're going to read it slowly, like she wanted. She'll be so happy!"

Lucy slipped on her flower-powers and followed her. "I'm going to go home to tell my mom some news—about my staying on Catalina this summer."

Lucy smiled to herself, warmth spreading through her entire body. "I have a feeling she'll be very happy, too."

The Lord himself will go before you.
He will be with you.
He will not leave you or forget you.
Don't be afraid. Don't worry.

DEUTERONOMY 31:8

SANDRA BYRD really *did* write in a diary when she was in sixth grade. It was a green leather one with a lock and key (which her little brother broke). She still has it. Maybe she'll hide it someplace good and see who finds it someday.

Sandra lives near beautiful Seattle, between the snow-capped Mount Rainier and the Space Needle, with her husband and two children (and let's not forget her Australian Shepherd, Trudy). When she's not writing, she's usually reading, but she also likes to scrapbook, listen to music, and spend time with friends. Besides writing THE HIDDEN DIARY books, she's also the author of the bestselling series SECRET SISTERS.

For more information on THE HIDDEN DIARY series, visit Sandra's Web site: *www.thehiddendiary.com.*

**Don't miss book two
of THE HIDDEN DIARY,
Just Between Friends!**

For a preview of Lucy and Serena's next diary adventure, just hold up this page in front of a mirror.

What happens when it's the last birthday before you're a teenager and you might get to have a party for once? Will anyone show up? And who sent that mean note, after all?